TEMPLE OF DAGON

AUTHOR: James Thomas	**ART DIRECTOR:** Casey Christofferson	**CARTOGRAPHY:** Robert Altbauer
EDITOR: Jeff Harkness	**LAYOUT:** Suzy Moseby	**FRONT COVER ART:** Artem Shukaev
SWORDS & WIZARDRY CONVERSION: Jeff Harkness	**INTERIOR ART:** Hector Rodriguez and Thuan Pham	**COVER DESIGN:** Casey Christofferson
	ART FOR VIRTUAL ASSETS: Brandon Sanderson	
	ONLINE PLATFORMS DEVELOPMENT: Sean King	

NECROMANCER
Games™

NECROMANCER Games

ISBN: 978-1-6656-0194-8
SW PoD

TABLE OF CONTENTS

Temple of Dagon 4

Adventure Background 4

Adventure Summary 4

A Profitable Proposal 4

The Sea Voyage 5

Santhera 5

Events in Santhera 5

  Bounty 6

  Recent Emissaries 6

  Piratical Conspiracy 6

  The Fang in the Sea 6

The Observatory Spire 7

  S-1. Observatory 7

  S-2. Divination Chamber 7

  S-3. Central Equipment Storage 7

The Observatory Spire Map 8

  S-4. Scriptorium 9

  S-5. Dormitory 9

  S-6. Entrance Hall 9

The Lost City 10

The Sunken Ruins 10

  R-1. Mall Prison 11

Mall Prison Map 12

  R-2. The Hag Garden 12

  R-3. Shrine of Insanity 12

The Hag Garden Map 13

  R-4. Doomsday Runes 14

Optional Sunken Ruin Dangers 14

Collapsing Building 14

Falling Block Trap 14

Explosive Glyph 14

Temple of Dagon 15

  T-1. Portico 15

  T-2. Entryway 15

  T-3. High Priestess's Room 15

    Wicked Reconfiguration Machine 15

  T-4. Priest Dormitory 16

Temple Map 16

  T-5. Sanctuary of Dagon 17

Lower Level Map 17

  T-6. Vertical Descent Passage 18

  T-7. Oratorium 18

  T-8. Ministry of Dagon 19

  T-9. Arcane Spell Chamber 19

    The Foul Chamber 19

  T-10. Skum Barracks 19

  T-11. Litharium 19

  T-12. Pilgrims' Hostel 20

  T-13. Guard Post 20

  T-14. Guest Room 20

  T-15. Underwater Approach 20

Epilogue 20

Appendix A: New Monsters 22

  Allip 22

  Assassin Vine 22

  Caryatid Column 22

  Cnidarian 23

Crystal Ooze 23
Devilfish 23
Eye of the Deep 24
Giant Blowfish 24
Giant Leech 24
Giant Moray Eel 24
Giant Sea Anemone, Immature 24
Gray Nisp 25
Skum 25
Swarm of Trilobites 25
Appendix B: Equipment & Magic Items 26
Miscellaneous Magical Items, Greater 26
Carpet of Holding 26
Decanter of Endless Air 26
Helm of Water Breathing 26
Miscellaneous Magical Item, Medium 26
Pearl of the Sirens 26
Missile Weapon 26
Arrow of Dragon Slaying 26
Potions 26
Potion of Barnacleskin 26
Potion of Fins to Feet 26
Potion of Water Breathing 26
Shield 26
Octopus Shield 26
Handout 27

TEMPLE OF DAGON

By James Thomas

A Swords & Wizardry adventure for 4–6 characters of 4th to 6th level

TEMPLE OF DAGON

A *Swords & Wizardry* adventure for 4–6 characters of 4th to 6th level

ADVENTURE BACKGROUND

Some knowledge is unfit for man. Yet ever have there been those who seek out the forbidden — the depraved — for the promise of riches and power. Terrible secrets can thus lie in the dark for generations before the foolhardy and ambitious unearth them once again. So too the wizards of the ancient world had among them those who were too ambitious and too unwise. When a cabal of these arcane philosophers migrated afar to establish a research colony apart from their countrymen, they abandoned all remaining restraint against forbidden lore. Their city grew, surrounded by other communities, and included an astrological and religious center several miles away.

Seduced by the promise of secret knowledge and power, they made pacts with wicked beings from beyond this mortal world. But this came at a price. They lost their humanity — morally and even physically — and their colony was destroyed. All the surrounding communities were dragged down with them. Their once great city of Atrotiri now lies wrecked where it sank beneath the waves of the Sinnar Ocean, an all but forgotten legend.

The small settlement of Santhera arose near the site of the disaster. Over the centuries, valuables were salvaged from the waters near the city. The temple site, however, lay unexplored until recently, when a sea medusa named Lycinia made herself mistress of the temple. A devotee of the demon lord Dagon, she sensed the ancient sacredness of the site and re-consecrated the temple to the worship of the "Shadow in the Sea." While exploring a nearby abyss, she encountered a colony of decadent skum languishing in a bizarre underwater metropolis. Her impassioned sermons on the glories of Dagon awakened purpose within their primeval hearts, and they joined her crusade to spread his gospel across the waters. Soon, sinister sea denizens from far and wide arrived, drawn by the rising power of the temple and their hunger for blood. They lodge in the sunken ruins ringing the temple mount, brooding and plotting.

ADVENTURE SUMMARY

The Temple of Dagon is located off a remote island chain in the Sinnar Ocean, 30 miles southwest of the small town of Santhera. It is a dangerous area due to an unusually large gathering of monstrous sea creatures found there. News of this archaeological site — which may still hold ancient artifacts — recently reached a collector who hopes to acquire these valuable ancient treasures. He now seeks to hire adventurers to plunder the long-forgotten temple.

When the characters arrive in Santhera, they learn the location of the temple site — and more. They discover that a cult of Dagon led by a secret priesthood is now active in the area and that the cultists are preying on nearby fisherfolk. Local merfolk communities also fear a mysterious spire rising out of the sea near the temple. As the adventurers approach the site, they glimpse the ancient temple building cresting above the waves and the sunken ruins in the surrounding shallows. A sealed stone spire jutting above the water hides a malevolent occupant but also presents a secret and secure refuge from which the characters can stage their exploration of the ruins. Danger lurks everywhere, and the characters must choose their strategy while raiding the sunken ruins or assaulting the temple. The ruins hold a variety of wicked sea creatures, dangerous hazards, and rare treasures.

Characters must enter the temple sanctuary where they encounter Dagon-worshipping cultists and skum warriors now dedicated to the evil demon prince. They also discover a flesh-warping and soul-twisting infernal machine that, when skillfully used, grants a boon; however, in unskilled hands it can also cause a terrible change. An underwater well in the sanctuary plunges into dark passageways to the chambers of the high priestess, an undersea medusa with coral snake hair. She and her lacedon guards (aquatic ghouls) fight a three-dimensional battle in a waterfilled chamber.

If the heroes approach underwater, they might also enter via a hidden sea cave (**Area T-15**) where they encounter aquatic trolls and other evil sea creatures. Worse yet, a visiting black dragon awaits. Delving deeper, however, they might find a sealed vault holding a collection of gemstones left untouched for centuries. Rare underwater equipment, forbidden knowledge, valuable booty, unique treasures and magic items await the plunder! Can the heroes make wise use of what they discover? Or will they too be drawn into a tempting trap of avarice like the ancients of Atrotiri?

A PROFITABLE PROPOSAL

In the city of Castorhage (or another suitable city in your campaign world), a notorious treasure hunter named **Cadan Trevethan** recently learned of the ruins of the Temple of Dagon. He desperately wants to acquire any arts and valuables from the site, but he knows this expedition is beyond his abilities. He hopes an able group of adventurers might make the trek and return with anything of value.

Cadan Trevethan, Male Human Retired Cat Burglar (Thf7): HP 23; **AC** 6[13]; **Atk** short sword (1d6) or *+1 dagger* (1d4+1); **Move** 9; **Save** 9; **AL** C; **CL/XP** 7/600; **Special:** +2 save bonus vs. traps and magical devices, backstab (x2), read languages, thieving skills.

Thieving Skills: Climb 91%, Tasks/Traps 45%, Hear 5 in 6, Hide 40%, Silent 50%, Locks 40%.

Equipment: leather armor, *+1 dagger*, short sword, 2d6 gp.

To that end, he summons the characters (their reputation having preceded them) to a private meeting. Read the following:

Cadan promises to pay in gold and silver for any ancient art and writings the characters might uncover. This includes items and rubbings of bas-reliefs or inscriptions. Cadan provides a roll of waterproof parchment and a special grease marker (usable above and below water) to obtain these. He tells the characters he will negotiate the price of each piece individually once they return. Any other valuables they find are fair salvage, but he offers to negotiate rates if the characters desire to sell.

Cadan arranges transport for the characters aboard his ship, *The Hurricane*, to and from Santhera. He promises that **Captain Blithe** will inform them of their destination once they are underway. Privately, Cadan instructs Captain Blithe to keep far from any danger at the temple site; he doesn't want to risk *The Hurricane*, after all. Finally, the captain introduces the characters to **Jamal**, a young djinni. As Cadan's agent, Jamal is authorized to secure any valuables aboard *The Hurricane*. Jamal offers to swiftly fly recovered treasures to and from the ancient site to the ship while the characters explore the ruins.

Captain Blithe, Male Human Captain of *The Hurricane*: HP 45; AC 7[12]; **Atk** longsword (1d8); **Move** 12; **Save** 9; **AL** N; **CL/XP** 7/600; **Special:** none.
    Equipment: leather armor, longsword, 2d6 sp.

Jamal, Young Djinni: HD 5; AC 5[14]; **Atk** fist or weapon (1d8); **Move** 9 (fly 24); **Save** 12; **CL/XP** 7/600; **Special:** spell-like abilities, whirlwind (10ft diameter, fewer than 1HD swept away). (***Monstrosities*** 126)

Spell-like Abilities: at will—create objects, gaseous form, *invisibility*.

THE DJINNI BOY

At 223 years of age, Jamal is young by genie standards. He resembles a human boy of 12 years with a personality to match, though he somehow is blessed with a wisdom beyond such years. He is only human-sized and tends to avoid combat. He turns invisible and flies away to avoid danger. A thoughtful being by nature, he creates food and water to refresh the party if they run short of food, wine, or other mundane supplies.

Jamal will not suspect any treachery from the characters, which means they can easily hide some of the ancient items they might find at the ruined temple. Even if he finds out, he might not care as he has no affection for Cadan. In his spare time, he amuses himself with a small hookah that he uses to exhale weaves of multicolored mist to form dancing girls, sea serpents, and scenes from home. He has a *carpet of holding* (see **Appendix B: Equipment & Magic Items**) to help tote any valuables the characters want to transport from the ruins to the ship.

THE SEA VOYAGE

Add whatever excitement you want to the sea journey, including any sea monsters or random weather events. When you are ready, the characters finally arrive at Santhera.

SANTHERA

The town of Santhera is the only substantial settlement found in this remote area of the Sinnar Ocean. It is a town of about 3,000 people, the vast majority human with several hundred halflings and a smattering of elves and dwarves. When *The Hurricane* arrives, the characters see a platform at the mouth of the bay. A galley guides the ship safely into the harbor, avoiding the treacherous obstacles hiding under the surface.

Notable members of Santhera include High Judge Percutio Opavian, Captain of the Guard Marco Domi, and High Priest Sister Pas:

Percutio Opavian, Male Human High Judge: HP 33; AC 9[10]; **Atk** dagger (1d4); **Move** 9; **Save** 12; **AL** C; **CL/XP** 5/240; **Special:** none.
    Equipment: robes, dagger, 3d6 gp.

Marco Domi, Male Human Captain of the Guard (Ftr5): HP 31; AC 5[14]; **Atk** longsword (1d8+1); **Move** 12; **Save** 10; **AL** N; **CL/XP** 5/240; **Special:** +1 to hit and damage strength bonus, multiple attacks (5) vs. creatures with 1 or fewer HD.
    Equipment: chainmail, longsword.

Sister Pas, Female Human High Priestess of Quell (Clr6): HP 29; AC 4[15]; **Atk** heavy mace (1d6); **Move** 12; **Save** 10; **AL** L; **CL/XP** 6/400; **Special:** +2 save vs. paralysis and poison, banish undead, spells (2/2/1/1).
    Spells: 1st—*detect evil, protection from evil*; 2nd—*bless, hold person*; 3rd—*cure disease*; 4th—*neutralize poison*.
    Equipment: chainmail, shield, *staff of healing* (26 charges), heavy mace, holy symbol of Quell.

Thousands of years ago, the island where Santhera now sits was larger and home to the city of Atrotiri. Few specifics are known about Atrotiri, but lore suggests it was founded as a colony of exiled wizards searching for a peaceful bastion in which to research their arcane philosophy. Darker tales are built upon rumors that the Atrotiri performed foul experiments that led to their exile originally, and that they modified these experiments to twist and enslave the creatures of the deep. Whichever is true, all stories agree that Atrotiri was destroyed after the mages dug too deeply into forbidden arts and triggered a massive earthquake that caused much of the island to slide into the sea, leaving behind only the massive crater that now forms Santheran Bay.

The ruins of old Atrotiri now cover the floor of the bay. During extremely low tides, the tips of old bronze spires and the jagged tops of stone walls still peek above the waters, and rich coral and pearl beds cover the submerged ruins. As the island was repopulated over the centuries, locals raised their children to be strong swimmers, sending the best down to dive for treasures. Sometimes, divers find ancient artifacts that collectors, wizards, and their agents are eager to possess. Much of the rest of the economy is simple fishing.

Ostensibly ruled by a town council, the Opavian family has effectively ruled the town for generations. The family keeps a tight grip on the positions of high judge over the island and council leader by nominating their own children, nieces, or nephews before retiring from the posts. Santherans are deeply conservative, though in practice they are largely apathetic. They live quiet lives filled with daily work and seasonal festivals, during which they drink fermented olive juice, just as their parents and grandparents before them.

EVENTS IN SANTHERA

Characters can learn useful rumors and make allies around Santhera. Use any of the following encounters as the characters explore the city. You can roll randomly or choose an encounter, although you may want to include the **Fang in the Sea** encounter if the characters don't have their own means to operate underwater for long periods of time.

1d4	Encounter
12	Bounty
15	Recent Emissaries
18	Piratical Conspiracy
20	The Fang in the Sea

The characters find a notice posted in a public place (see the **bounty poster handout** at the end of the adventure). If they take the notice to the judicial palace, the characters soon find themselves before **High Judge Percutio Opavian**, who explains the situation and makes them an offer. Merchant vessels have gone missing of late, and indications are that the attacks originate at underwater ruins 30 miles from town. The high judge wants the area investigated immediately and offers a yearlong letter of marque to any adventurers willing to take the bounty. High Judge Opavian pays 50 gp in cash for useful information about the attacks plus an additional 10 gp for the head of each marauder "brought to justice" dead or alive. Santhera is not a wealthy community and cannot afford to pay much. If pressed for more, the high judge offers free provisions including food, ammunition (standard, nonmagical arrows, bolts, and sling bullets), and lodging in the Magocrat, the best (and only) inn in Santhera. Residents are unwilling to accompany the characters to the ruins, and the high judge cannot spare anyone to accompany them.

Captain Blithe will not take *The Hurricane* into hazards beyond Santhera under any circumstances, so the characters must find another way to the island. A bribe of 20 gp convinces a local fisherman named Fodor to guide them to the site in his small fishing boat, but he won't remain to wait for their return. The party can also purchase a used fishing boat for 50 gp if they have no other means of traveling the 30 miles across the sea.

The djinni Jamal will carry treasure to and from the ruins for them, but he won't assist the characters in getting there.

RECENT EMISSARIES

Local merfolk visited Santhera several weeks ago and reported that organized bands of sahuagin and other wicked sea denizens had launched raids on their outlying communities. The raiders were well-equipped and used strange magic. Scouting parties concluded that the raiders seemed to originate from the underwater ruins and the ancient temple. They can serve as guides to the temple and, if questioned, can identify the Fang in the Sea. They know very little about the temple, though they can introduce the characters to Namara. The merfolk avoid combat and hastily retreat if threatened or attacked.

Merfolk (as needed): HD 1; **AC** 7[12]; **Atk** trident (1d6) or short sword (1d6); **Move** 18 (swim); **Save** 17; **AL** Any; **CL/XP** 1/15; **Special:** breathe water. (*Monstrosities* 328)

PIRATICAL CONSPIRACY

The characters overhear the following conversation when they are in a crowded tavern or at the Magocrat.

> The voice of a fisherman near you draws your attention. He straddles a chair and faces away from you, conversing with a group of friends at his table. He drinks his fill and slams the mug down on the table before he speaks. "If you ask me, it's none other than the high judge behind the raids on the trade ships. He's enriching himself and his friends, depriving us and blaming it on outsiders."
>
> The patron to his right nods in agreement. "Aye, Dubio. Why do you think there's that strange ship in the harbor? *The Hurricane*? And those crude mercenaries stomping around? The judge is preparing to put down any resistance to his rule if word gets out that he's involved."

This is a false rumor. Although there certainly is corruption in the local government, the high judge is not responsible for the raids and genuinely desires to end the attacks lest the town's supplies suffer.

While gathering information, the characters encounter emissaries of **Namara**, who insists on meeting the whole party so she can share the following:

> "Since monsters destroyed my village 800 years ago, I have resided in a nearby merfolk village. The gods of the seafolk heard my desperate prayers and sent me a vision of off-islanders defeating the evil that attacked my people."

After sharing her story, she requests their help protecting her community. She tells them about the Fang in the Sea and asks them to expunge that evil. If they agree, she continues:

> "A black granite pinnacle juts from the sea 30 nautical miles southwest of Santhera. The fisherfolk call it the Fang in the Sea. It marks the periphery of the sunken remains of an ancient city lost long ago beneath the waves. Evil waits there."

Namara directs the characters to the spire or she accompanies them if asked, although she will not enter the temple. Namara is a helpful soul who can provide the characters with the means to explore the underwater ruins. She provides each character with a *pearl of the sirens* (see **Appendix B: Equipment & Magic Items**) if they vow to put to rest the troubled spirits of her former comrades trapped in the ruins. The magical pearls should allow the characters to travel freely in the underwater environment. She could also provide a *decanter of endless air* (see **Appendix B: Equipment & Magic Items**).

Namara, Female Elf Sea Priestess (Clr5): HP 22; **AC** 7[12]; **Atk** club (1d4); **Move** 9; **Save** 11; **AL** L; **CL/XP** 5/240; **Special:** +2 save vs. paralysis and poison, banish undead, spells (2/2).
    Spells: 1st—*cure light wounds, detect magic*; 2nd—*bless, hold person*.
Equipment: *helm of water breathing*, leather armor, club, silver necklace (summons a giant seahorse 1/week).

GETTING AROUND UNDER THE WAVES

After the characters leave Santhera, they are going to have to have some means of swimming and, more importantly, breathing, underwater. The Fang in the Sea encounter above allows you provide each character with a magical pearl so they can get around safe underwater. Alternately, you could allow the characters to purchase some of the magical items found in Appendix B: Equipment & Magic Items from vendors around the village. Set the price based on what the characters are able to pay in your campaign world.

THE OBSERVATORY SPIRE

An ancient temple to a forgotten god crests above the waves 30 nautical miles from Santhera, perched upon what must have been the highest hill in the former city. This is the location Cadan hired the characters to investigate. The spire is made of nearly seamless thick granite and has no obvious entrance.

However, if Namara accompanied the characters, she tells them that she was one of five adventurers who gained entrance to the spire long ago. Their astrologer Shalell and the historian Feloor found a doorway near the top of the spire and opened it one dark night almost 800 years ago. But she warns the characters of a terrible ghostly girl who slew her companions and turned them into evil spirits. Nevertheless, if the characters destroy the undead denizens, the shelter would be a secure place to rest between forays into the temple or the underwater ruins, for it is nigh impregnable.

At night, glowing runes on the side of the spire are visible by starlight or moonlight. The runes begin to glow one after another as the moon and stars rise. If each rune is traced in that same sequence, a stone doorway recedes inward and sinks into the floor to reveal an ornate star chamber. Once the pattern is known, the door can be opened day or night by retracing the runes. However, the outside runes and the opening are 10 feet above the sea's surface at high tide, so characters might need to climb or use some sort of magical assistance to reach them.

If Namara is still with the characters, she informs the characters how to open the door now that she has seen the runes again. Once the door is opened, she avoids combat and refuses under any conditions to enter the tower. If monsters attack, she jumps into the water, summons a giant seahorse with her necklace, and flees.

THE OBSERVATORY SPIRE'S HISTORY

Jorell the Stargazer locked his young daughter, Ismene (*iz'-meh-nay*), in the tower to protect her from the disaster he knew would befall the city. Alas, his inattention over the years had already planted seeds of bitterness that their abrupt parting caused to spring up full blown, paying tragic dividends. After the city sank, killing nearly everyone including her whole family, Ismene was left all alone and unable to escape the observatory spire. As the darkness closed in, she gave in to her bitterness and anger, blaming her father for her predicament and for every awful thing that had ever happened to her. She smashed every object she could find, tore up books, and damaged furniture. In the end, still bitter and resentful, she died of hunger and became a terrible spectre. The spire also contains her three spawn (spectres), undead corruptions of Namara's companions who entered the spire long ago.

The spire, one of the most revered buildings in the ancient city, is quite solidly built and completely intact. Presently, the interior is unlit unless otherwise stated. The floors, walls, and ceilings are made of dark granite and ornate marble. Amazingly, most furnishings are still in one piece. If cleared of evil spirits, this ancient building could indeed provide a safe and secure hideout for the adventurers. If they are careful not to be observed withdrawing to this location, the temple's denizens may never find them. And even if the characters are seen, their foes have no way of getting inside (none knows the secret of tracing the runes). Even Jamal the djinni can't enter the spire unless it is opened for him. The characters can use the crystal sphere in the divination chamber (**Area S-2**) to view the outside world to see who's there. They can open the door from the inside at any time, day or night.

S-1. OBSERVATORY

Precise gaps in the stone lattice above allow viewers to track the movement of various stars and constellations, measure the passage of time, take astrological readings, and view portents from beyond. The room is otherwise vacant.

A secret counterweight and lever allow those inside the chamber to open and close the observatory's door from the inside. It takes two rounds to close and seal the spire. Besides opening and closing the secret entrance, the ancient astrologers could also retract and close openings in the walls and roof, and even rotate them to align the room with a variety of celestial constellations. The devices for these movements are missing, however, and the magical energies that powered them are long dormant.

The hole in the middle of the floor is all that remains of a magical elevator that ran from the top of the spire to the bottom. A stone levitating table the ancients stood upon now lies in pieces at the bottom of the shaft. The descent to the level below therefore requires a character to jump, fly, use magic, or descend by rope. It's a 15-foot drop to the next floor down. A character who fails a saving throw when dropping down lands successfully but falls prone and takes 1d6 points of damage. A character who fails the save by 5 or more misses the edge of the floor below and falls to the bottom of the shaft, taking 1d6 points of damage per 10 feet fallen. Each level is 15 feet from floor to floor and the fall alerts the monsters on each level as the character goes past.

Loud noises in this area attract monsters in the room below.

S-2. DIVINATION CHAMBER

Lurking here are **3 spectres**. Ismene gave them names: Bitterness, Envy, and Vengeance. If they hear voices from the floor above, they fly up to attack. Otherwise, they hide in the walls and try to forget the undead horrors they have become.

The last intact globe is three feet wide and filled with pure elemental water. Spellcasters can use it as a scrying device that operates as a *crystal ball*. It is encased in its metal stand, which is attached to the floor. Removing it is impossible without breaking it. No other valuables are in this room.

Bitterness, Envy, and Vengeance, Spectres (3): HD 6; **HP** 43, 39, 32; **AC** 2[17]; **Atk** spectral weapon or touch (1d8 + level drain); **Move** 15 (fly 30); **Save** 11; **AL** C; **CL/XP** 9/1100; **Special:** +1 or better magic weapons to hit, level drain (2 levels with hit). (*Monstrosities* 445)

S-3. CENTRAL EQUIPMENT STORAGE

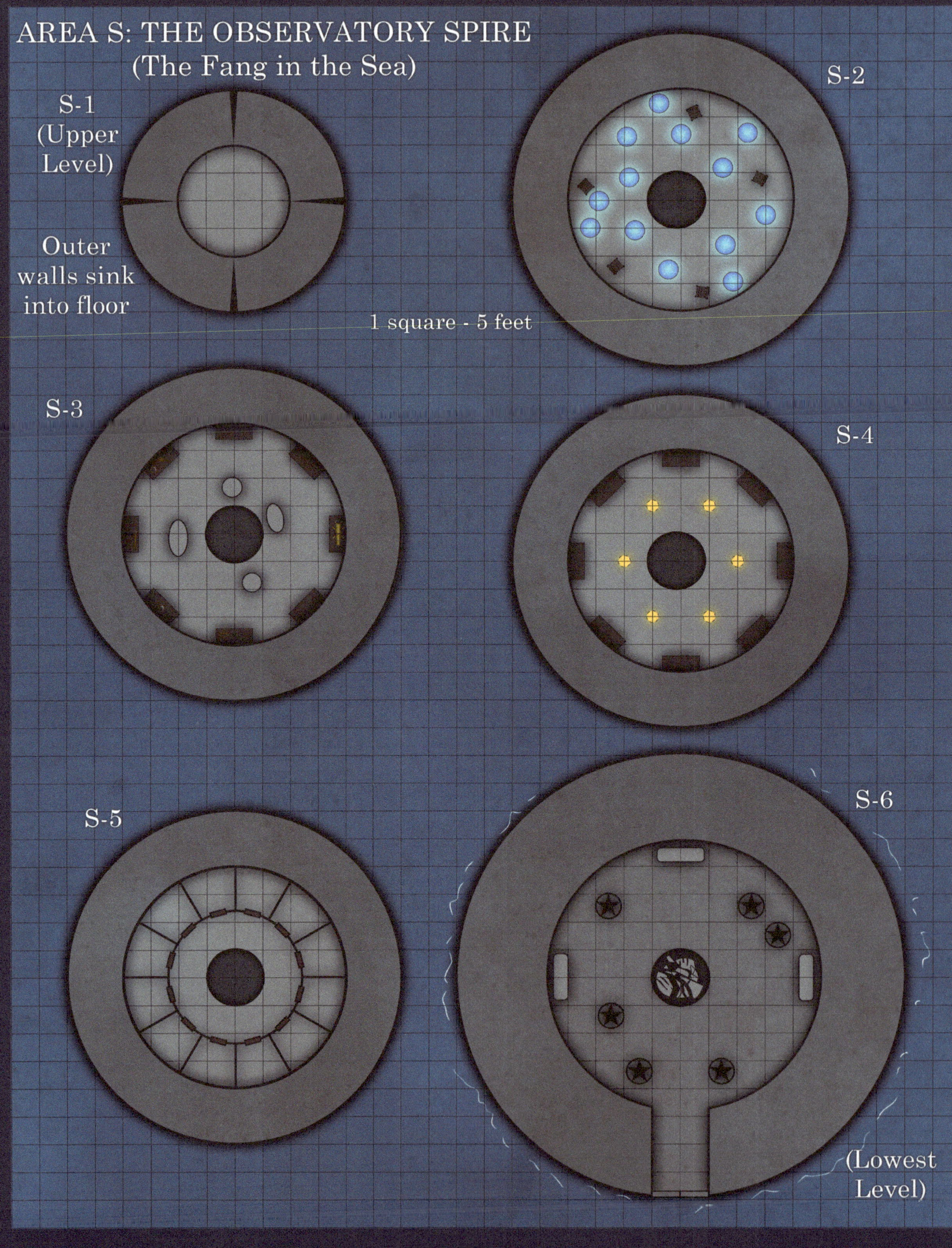

AREA S: THE OBSERVATORY SPIRE
(The Fang in the Sea)
S-1
(Upper
Level)
Outer
walls sink
into floor
1 square - 5 feet
S-2
S-3
S-4
S-5
S-6
(Lowest
Level)

A variety of astrological instruments are in this room, from magnifying glasses to telescopes, and compasses to astrolabes. There are tools for basic maintenance and spare lenses and other parts in handy drawers. The ancient artifacts found here are worth 12,000 gp, and Jamal happily receives them as recovered "art."

S-4. SCRIPTORIUM

Ornate bookshelves and crisscrossing shelves line the walls of this room from floor to ceiling. Shredded paper is strewn all over the floor. Above, ever-burning light globes dangling from ornate brass chains fill the room with soft illumination. Other smaller lights extend from the walls on scissor brackets across shelving and above stuffed chairs.

For this encounter, identify five or six squares of rough terrain on the map to represent the chaos of Ismene's angry rampage so many centuries ago. Strangely afraid of the intruders, the **spectre Ismene** hides inside a random bookcase. She flies into a rage and attacks if she hears a man's voice, as this reminds her of her hated father.

Most of the books here are on scrolls, and most of them were torn to shreds long ago. They are all written in ancient languages from more than 3,000 years ago. No magic books or scrolls are present, but the ancient writings that can be recovered are worth 9,000 gp. Ismene's physical remains — a girl's emaciated body — are huddled in a corner.

Ismene, Spectre: HD 6; **HP** 47; **AC** 2[17]; **Atk** spectral weapon or touch (1d8 + level drain); **Move** 15 (fly 30); **Save** 11; **AL** C; **CL/XP** 9/1100; **Special:** +1 or better magic weapons to hit, level drain (2 levels with hit). (**Monstrosities** 445)

S-5. DORMITORY

Three apartments cluster at each of the four compass points, for a total equaling the sacred number 12. Each has a wooden door and a bronze latch and lock. None is locked.

A key hangs behind each door on a cloak hook. A simple bed with a mattress on a bronze bed frame is inside each cell. A chamber pot is beneath each mattress. An ever-burning lantern hangs from the ceiling on a bronze chain. The lantern can be opened and closed to provide bright, dim, or no light. A desk and chair sit in one corner. Otherwise, each room is empty.

S-6. ENTRANCE HALL

This gorgeous entrance hall displays ornate marble on every surface, including statuesque bas-reliefs festooning the walls and ceiling. A pile of stone rubble rests in the middle of the room below a hole in the ceiling above it. Fifteen-foot-tall doors of plain black stone loom on one side of the chamber.

The stone doors can be opened only after disabling the lock in the wall by the side of the door and then pulling a lever. Opening the door is a grave error for the fool who does so, however. As the stone doors recedes into the floor, water gushes into the tower with great force, flooding **Areas S-3** through **S-6** and filling half of **Area S-2**. Each creature in the room takes 3d6 points of damage, or half as much with a successful saving throw.

THE LOST CITY

The core of this adventure takes place at the temple, but enterprising players may want to explore around the underwater ruins for monsters and treasure. Make the ruins as elaborate or as simple as desired depending on the interests of your gaming group. Mark which encounters you wish to include and keep a tally of what monsters remain. Rather than having them quit the region, the surviving monsters could flee to the temple to be encountered anew in the pilgrims' hostel (**Area T-12**).

As much of the rest of the adventure takes place underwater, the characters will need some method of breathing and moving below the waves. The characters might have their own abilities (from Namara or purchased other magical items in Santhera as described above) or you could sprinkle some items in the observatory or the ruins for them to find. Visibility is quite good in these clear waters, so the only restrictions are light and obstacles. Almost all the monsters here are aquatic. Remember the three-dimensional aspect of the environment enables attacks to come from above and below.

THE SUNKEN RUINS

Below are four encounter areas that can be placed anywhere in the sunken ruins. Choose encounters that allow your players to show off their characters' special abilities and keep them interested in the adventure. You don't have to use them all, but if you want more, you can use the **Random Sunken Ruins Encounters** table below to spice things up. The shallow seawaters here range between 20 to 60 feet below the surface. During the day, the water is clear enough that characters can see the ruined buildings about 40 feet below the surface. You could use any convenient city street maps you have handy and dress them up as ruins. Players may enjoy having their characters swim over walls and rooftops on previously used flip maps. Organize encounters in the sunken ruin by placing encounters where they make sense to you. The remainder of the ruins should be empty shells of buildings or rubble.

Monsters in the ruins are awaiting their next marauding mission, but they attack if they detect intruders. Swimming or boating in plain sight is a good way to get clobbered by the bad guys. If the party takes reasonable precautions to avoid being detected by residents of the ruins, reward them with limited or no random encounters. If, however, they boldly and blatantly swoop in like flying superheroes, they have chosen a path of pain. Use the **Random Sunken Ruins Encounters** table below and show no mercy as the denizens below spot them and attack. As more monsters get word of the characters' presence, they attack in waves and alert the temple for backup. You obviously don't want to punish your players if they realize too late what they've gotten into. The game can still be saved; as things heat up, give them hints and opportunities to retreat and regroup. Remind them that they were told this area is likely a hub of the recent attacks and that monsters are certainly lurking in the ruins.

Random Sunken Ruins Encounters

1d12	Result
1	1d4 caryatid column guardians
2	3 skum warriors
3	1d6+2 skum pilgrims
4	2d4 sahuagin
5	Crystal ooze
6	Spirit naga (aquatic)
7	1d4 allips (ghosts of the ancient city)
8	Storm giant (evil, Dagon-worshipping)
9	1d4 lacedons (aquatic ghouls)
10	2 aquatic trolls
11	3 Dagon priests
12	Eye of the deep

Allips (1d4): HD 4; AC 5[14]; **Atk** strike (no damage, drain wisdom); **Move** 6 (fly); **Save** 13; **AL** C; **CL/XP** 7/600; **Special:** +1 or better magic or silver weapon to hit, drain wisdom (1d4 points with hit), hypnosis (as *suggestion* spell). (see **Appendix A: New Monsters**)

Caryatid Columns (1d4): HD 5; AC 5[14]; **Atk** longsword (1d8+1); **Move** 9; **Save** 12; **AL** N; **CL/XP** 7/600; **Special:** immune to magic (except *transmute rock to mud* [1d6 damage per level], *transmute mud to rock* [heals all damage], *stone to flesh* [subject to normal damage and magic for 1 round]), resist normal weapons (50%

damage), shatter weapons (weapon that hits must save or be destroyed). (see **Appendix A: New Monsters**)

Crystal Ooze: HD 4; AC 7[12]; **Atk** strike (2d6 + paralysis); **Move** 3 (swim 6); **Save** 13; **AL** N; **CL/XP** 6/400; **Special:** acid (dissolve organic material), immunities (acid, cold, fire), paralysis (save or paralyzed for 3d6 rounds), transparent (20% chance to spot in water), water dependent (dies after five hours out of water). (see **Appendix A: New Monsters**)

Eye of the Deep: HD 10; AC 4[15]; **Atk** 2 pincers (2d4 + constrict), bite (1d6); **Move** 3 (swim 9); **Save** 5; **AL** C; **CL/XP** 13/2300; **Special:** constrict (after pincer hit, save or held, automatic 2d4 damage per round, Open Doors check to escape), eye rays (attack as 12th-level caster, ranged attack to hit, 150ft range, 1 each/round [*hold person, hold monster*] or 1/round [*phantasmal force*]), stun cone (central eye, 30ft cone, 1/round [save or stunned for 2d4 rounds]). (see **Appendix A: New Monsters**)

Lacedons (Aquatic Ghouls) (1d4): HD 2; AC 6[13]; **Atk** 2 claws (1d3 + paralysis), bite (1d4); **Move** 9 (swim 12); **Save** 16; **AL** C; **CL/XP** 3/60; **Special:** immunities (charm and sleep), paralyzing touch (3d6 turns, save avoids). (*Monstrosities* 191)

Priests of Dagon, Male or Female Humans or Elves (Clr4) (3): HP 4d6; AC 7[12]; **Atk** flail (1d8); **Move** 12; **Save** 12; **AL** C; **CL/XP** 4/120; **Special:** +2 save vs. paralysis and poison, banish undead, darkvision (60ft) (elves only), spells (2/1).
Spells: 1st—*cure light wounds* (x2); 2nd—*hold person*.
Equipment: leather armor, flail, holy symbol of Dagon.

Sahuagins (2d4): HD 2+1; AC 5[14]; **Atk** weapon (1d8); **Move** 12 (swim 18); **Save** 16; **AL** C; **CL/XP** 2/30; **Special:** none. (*Monstrosities* 407)

Skum (1d6+2): HD 3; AC 5[14]; **Atk** trident (1d6) or 2 claws (1d4), bite (2d4); **Move** 9 (swim 12); **Save** 14; **AL** C; **CL/XP** 3/60; **Special:** none. (see **Appendix A: New Monsters**)

Skum Warriors (3): HD 5; AC 3[16]; **Atk** *+1 trident* (1d6+1) or 2 claws (1d6), bite (2d4); **Move** 9 (swim 12); **Save** 12; **AL** C; **CL/XP** 5/240; **Special:** none. (see **Appendix A: New Monsters**)
Equipment: *+1 trident, potion of extra healing.*

Spirit Naga: HD 9; AC 5[14]; **Atk** bite (1d3 + poison); **Move** 12; **Save** 6; **AL** C; **CL/XP** 13/2300; **Special:** charm gaze (as *charm person*), lethal poison (save or die), spells (MU 4/2/1; Clr 2/1). (*Monstrosities* 344)

Storm Giant: HD 15+5; AC 1[18]; **Atk** weapon (7d6); **Move** 15; **Save** 3; **AL** Any; **CL/XP** 16/3200; **Special:** throw boulders (7d6), control weather (as spell). (*Monstrosities* 201)

Trolls, Aquatic (2): HD 6+3; AC 4[15]; **Atk** 2 claws (1d4), bite (1d8); **Move** 12; **Save** 11; **AL** C; **CL/XP** 8/800; **Special:** amphibious, regenerate (3hp/round). (*Monstrosities* 489)

R-1. Mall Prison

Read the following if the characters enter:

This two-story complex was once part of a vast indoor bazaar. Now, the shops are makeshift cells for captives taken in recent raids. The central passage is 30 feet wide and 70 feet long before it makes a sharp turn that ends in rubble. Cells are located every 10 feet or so along the passage. The ruined roof is mostly intact but a search

from above the building reveals an opening in the back around the eastern corner where characters could sneak inside.

Manning this area at all times are **10 skum**, with two at the entryway and the remainder at the back. They are bored with their duties and fill the empty hours with an underwater ballgame called "lathoosh," a three-player game with racquets and a ball very much like a mix of lacrosse and tennis. They also enjoy terrorizing the merfolk with monstrous eels. Thus, they may be unaware of approaching characters if they quietly slay the two skum at the entrance. If hard pressed, they release the eels to join the fight.

The net contains **2 giant moray eels**. They attack if one of the prison guards releases them. Awaiting their fate as blood sacrifices to Dagon are **14 merfolk** who are attached to the walls by bronze shackles. One of them, Jahwass, is of noble birth. A reward arrives at Santhera for the characters three days after his safe return: a box of rare pearls (2,000 gp) and a *+2 trident*. A locked box nearby holds the merfolk equipment and weapons. The keys to the manacles and strongbox hang on a peg near the entrance.

Skum (10): HD 3; HP 21, 19x2, 17, 14, 13x3, 10, 8; AC 5[14]; **Atk** trident (1d6) or 2 claws (1d4), bite (2d4); **Move** 9 (swim 12); **Save** 14; **AL** C; **CL/XP** 3/60; **Special:** none. (see **Appendix A: New Monsters**)

Giant Moray Eels (2): HD 4; HP 27, 23; AC 7[12]; **Atk** bite (2d6); **Move** 0 (swim 9); **Save** 13; **AL** N; **CL/XP** 4/120; **Special:** none. (see **Appendix A: New Monsters**)

Merfolk (14): HD 1; HP 2 each; AC 7[12]; **Atk** weapon (1d6); **Move** 18 (swim); **Save** 17; **AL** Any; **CL/XP** 1/15; **Special:** breathe water. (*Monstrosities* 328)

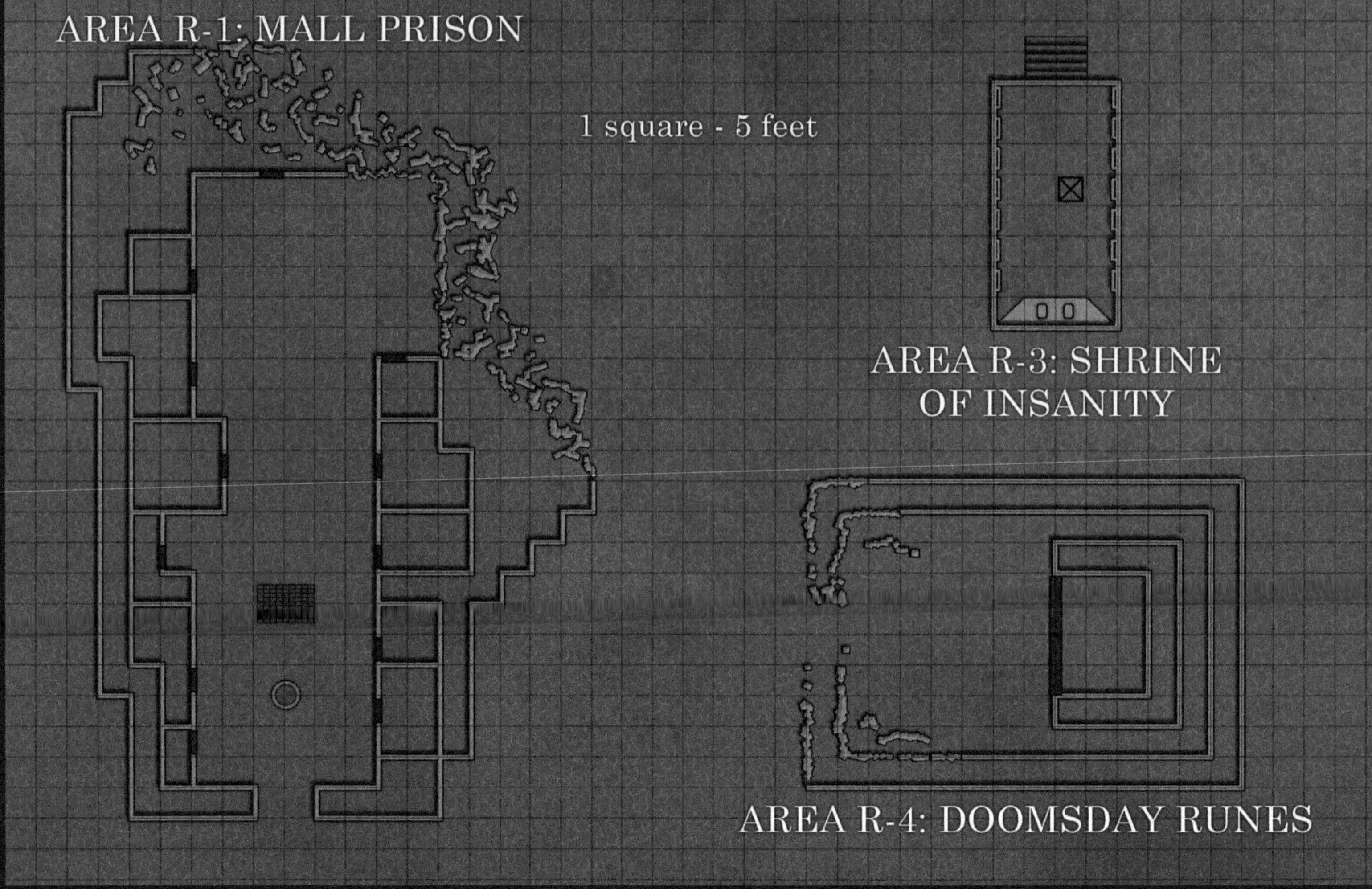

R-2. The Hag Garden

A bizarre garden of undersea fauna and flora adorn what must have once been a stately promenade of monuments and columns. The plants are a riot of color and ghastly themes. Pairs of merfolk in gaudy costumes stroll along the promenade, seemingly enjoying the scenery. Statues of petrified sailors and merfolk in grim and horrified poses dot the landscape as schools of zombie fish meander drearily in a circuit from one end of the garden to the other. Ancient statuary surround a large fountain spurting fine, white sand that cascades down like rivulets. An undead octopus propels the sand from beneath the fountain.

A coven of **3 sea hags** constructed this garden of monstrous flora to amuse themselves. They consider it high art and are quite conceited about their creation. All the creatures therein obey their commands. The cavorting merfolk are actually **6 zombie merfolk** covered by illusions. They continue their circuit from one end of the garden to the other and merely smile and nod to any who address them. The groves on either side of the garden each contain a patch of monstrous kelp (as **assassin vines**) that attack those who stray too close (reach five feet). Throughout the garden are **4 giant immature sea anemones** that attack creatures as large as the characters only if a hag commands them to do so. Several varieties of poisonous undersea plants are carefully cultivated here for nefarious purposes. Address these only if the characters take interest in them. The hags are protective of their garden and attack intruders, calling to the zombies to assist them. The zombies attempt to herd creatures into the grasp of the anemones and the assassin vines.

The animated dead fish swim about for artistic effect and are not dangerous enough to count as a monster. The octopus zombie could be an easy kill as the characters are searching for treasure as it does not stop operating the fountain.

Sea Hags (3): HD 3; HP 23, 21, 19; AC 6[13]; **Atk** bite (1d4); **Move** 6 (swim 18); **Save** 14; **AL** C; **CL/XP** 5/240; **Special:** death gaze (3/day, 30ft range, save or die), weakness gaze (save or strength reduce by half for 1d6 turns). (***Monstrosities*** 239)

Assassin Vines (Kelp): HD 7; AC 5[14]; **Atk** vine (1d6+1); **Move** 1; **Save** 9; **AL** N; **CL/XP** 8/800; **Special:** animate plants (30ft range, immobilize any creature that fails a saving throw). (***Monstrosities*** 23)

Sea Anemones (4): HD 8; HP 56, 50, 43, 39; AC 8[11]; **Atk** tendrils (paralysis); **Move** 0 (immobile); **Save** 8; **AL** N; **CL/XP** 8/800; **Special:** acid cloud (1d8 damage for 1d3 rounds to all within 20 feet radius), paralytic poison (save or immobilized), swallow whole (immobilized creatures). (***Monstrosities*** 21)

The hags have the following valuables on their persons: a bag of 20 adamantine sling bullets, a *potion of gaseous form*, a *potion of water breathing* (see **Appendix B: Equipment & Magic Items**), and a *potion of clairvoyance*. Three of the merfolk wear valuable jewelry (total value 600 gp). If the fountain area is searched, a giant oyster is found behind the fountain. This three-foot-wide mollusk is not dangerous, but if pried open, a valuable pearl is found within (700 gp). Lastly, three silver coins are in the fountain.

R-3. Shrine of Insanity

This shrine to a forgotten alien god bears a terrible curse. The skum marked the underground entrance with a warning sign: two driftwood planks formed into an "X" with a downward pointing scallop shell in the middle, the skum sign for "Danger! Do not enter!"

A slimy 10-foot-wide stairway steeply descends into darkness before emerging at last in a cold, water-filled chamber dimly illuminated by green glowing eyes of grotesque carvings that run the length of what must have been a small underground temple. A steep pit is in the middle of the floor. A golden idol of a bull-headed man covered in jewels sits on a dais at the far end of the shrine.

AREA R-2: THE HAG GARDEN
1 square - 5 feet
Street
Fountain
Kelp
Kelp
Street
Alley
Promenade
Alley
Ruins
Street
Ruins
Sea grass
Sea grass
Ruins
Ruins
Ruined Palace
Statue
Anemone

The temple chamber is 20 feet wide, 10 feet high, and 40 feet long. The area is bare except for the seven-foot-tall golden idol at the rear of the sanctuary. The pit in the middle of the room is an old trap sprung long ago by a looter whose skeletal remains lie amid broken tiles 40 feet down. A **gibbering mouther** slumbers under rubble in a corner of the pit. It is sensitive to vibrations and awakens and attacks immediately if the rubble or bones are disturbed. A second **gibbering mouther** dozes behind the statue but awakens and attacks if it detects noises or bright light.

Gibbering Mouthers (2): HD 8; HP 60, 52; AC 1[18]; **Atk** 6 mouths (1d4 + attach + pull prey underneath); **Move** 3; **Save** 8; **AL** C; **CL/ XP** 10/1400; **Special:** attach (automatic 1d4 bite damage per round after hit), gibbering (60ft radius, as *confusion* spell, save avoids), spit (20ft range, save or blinded for 1 round), pull prey underneath (5% chance after bite, additional 5% per mouth attached, automatic 12d4 damage, save for half). (*Monstrosities* 203)

Anyone touching the idol feels a vibration thrum through their body and must succeed on a saving throw or fall under a terrible curse. The cursed creature assumes an amorphous, shapeless mass. Its body melts and flows, leaving the creature unable to hold or use any item such as weapons, clothing, armor, helmets, and rings. The affected creature's movement is reduced by half and it cannot cast spells or use magic items. It attacks blindly and cannot distinguish friend from foe.

The target must make a saving throw each round. A failed saving throw means the creature takes 1d6 points of damage per round until it "dies," at which point it transforms over four agonizing rounds into a gibbering mouther with full hit points. Only *resurrection* or *limited wish* can reverse the transformation once it is complete.

A successful saving throw lets the creature resume its normal form for one minute and avoid taking damage during that time. In addition, spells such as *polymorph self* or *polymorph other* let the creature retain its shape for the duration of the spell. *Remove curse* has a 5 percent chance per level of the caster of removing the curse entirely.

If the idol is pulled down, it smashes into several pieces on the floor. The idol is hollow with clay over a metal frame. The evil magic is no longer a danger. The small body of a long-dead young person is found inside the statue. Based on the construction, this was a sacrifice who died horribly to consecrate the idol when the clay was fired. The gold leaf covering the outside is difficult to recover and not worth much (50 gp). The rubies and emeralds covering the idol are worth 5,200 gp.

R-4. Doomsday Runes

As the characters continue through the ruins, a blue glow pulses in the waters around them as they pass a crumbling building. Read the following:

A blue glow from the ruins of a nearby building softly illuminates the underwater city. The light pulses like a beating heart that ripples the still waters.

The otherwise nondescript building contains a sizable stone object covered in ancient runes. *Read languages* reveals the words "guardian" and "protection" in the jumble of symbols. One side of the stone has a flat palm-size indentation discolored from use. If a character foolishly places his or her hand in the indentation, the runes on the stone illuminate and hum. Doing so activates an ancient city guardian tasked to destroy intruders. Since no citizens are left to control the guardian, it targets every living thing in sight. With one last pulse of intense blue light, the front of the stone block swings open, and the **stone golem** inside attacks immediately. The construct pursues characters beyond this building but it cannot swim, which should make this an easier encounter for clever players. Rubbings of the runes are worth 2,000 gp.

Stone Golem: HD 12; HP 60; AC 5[14]; **Atk** fist (3d8); **Move** 6; **Save** 3; **CL/XP** 16/3200; **Special:** +2 or better magic weapon to hit, immune to most magic (slowed by fire, damaged by rock to mud). (*Monstrosities* 222)

Optional Sunken Ruin Dangers

If you need more encounters in the sunken ruins, the following list of dangers can enhance the **Random Sunken Ruins Encounters**:

Collapsing Building

Some ruined buildings may be dangerously unstable. Characters have a 1-in-6 chance to spot a weakened ceiling. A creature beneath the ceiling when a loud noise or explosion occurs must make a saving throw. The creature takes 3d6 points of damage and is buried on a failure, or half as much and is not buried on a success. A buried creature takes 1d6 points of damage each round until freed. A buried creature can attempt an Open Doors check to get free, or a nearby creature can do the same.

Falling Block Trap

A pressure plate or tripwire triggers a 10-foot-square block of stone to fall. Each creature in the area when the block falls must succeed on a saving throw or take 3d6 points of damage and be restrained by the block. A creature can free itself with by rolling below its strength on 4d6. An adjacent creature can do the same. The trigger for the trap can be detected and disarmed with thieves' tools.

Explosive Glyph

A creature passing through a doorway triggers a magical glyph that erupts with energy in a 20-foot-radius sphere centered on the glyph. The sphere spreads around corners. Each creature in the area takes 6d6 points of damage, or half as much if they make a saving throw. Characters who investigate the doorway before entering can find the glyph.

TEMPLE OF DAGON

T-1. Portico

Most areas are slime-covered and slippery. At night, **2 skum** temple guards on opposite porticos watch for interlopers. By day, **2 priests** keep watch instead (see **Area T-4**). Neither pair tries to conceal themselves, so the party might spot them in time to eliminate the sentinels by stealth. If the guards detect a dangerous group approaching, they warn the guards and priests inside to prepare. If you really want to increase the challenge, **2 devilfish** attack from underwater as the party tops the landing. The clamor of combat likely betrays the party's presence and delays their entrance into the temple proper. It also increases the chances that one of the sentinels rushes in and alerts the defenders.

Priests of Dagon, Male or Female Humans or Elves (Clr4) (2): HP 21, 18; **AC** 7[12]; **Atk** flail (1d8); **Move** 12; **Save** 12; **AL** C; **CL/XP** 4/120; **Special:** +2 save vs. paralysis and poison, banish undead, darkvision (60ft) (elves only), spells (2/1).
  Spells: 1st—*cure light wounds* (x2); 2nd—*hold person.*
Equipment: leather armor, flail, holy symbol of Dagon
Skum (2): HD 3; HP 20, 18; **AC** 5[14]; **Atk** trident (1d6) or 2 claws (1d4), bite (2d4); **Move** 9 (swim 12); **Save** 14; **AL** C; **CL/XP** 3/60; **Special:** none. (see **Appendix A: New Monsters**)
Devilfish (2): HD 5; HP 36, 30; **AC** 5[14]; **Atk** 3 tentacles (1d6+2 + grapple), bite (2d6+2); **Move** 3 (swim 15); **Save** 12; **AL** C; **CL/XP** 6/400; **Special:** grapple (save after strike or held, automatic bite damage until freed), resists cold (50% damage), unholy blood (1/day, emit cloud, 20ft radius, save or poisoned, –2 to hit, saves, and damage for 1d6 rounds). (see **Appendix A: New Monsters**)

T-2. Entryway

This level of the temple is not underwater. The ceiling height is 30 feet. The underwater portion of this complex begins beneath the sanctuary of Dagon (**Area T-5**). The water in the pool is one-foot deep and contains unholy water. Lawful creatures who touch the water take 1d4 points of damage per round. They take 2d6 points of damage if submerged in the water. The sea nymph statue is made of gilded green marble and holds a bronze bow and arrow. Close scrutiny reveals that the arrow is not a part of the statue. It is in fact an *arrow of dragon slaying* (see **Appendix B: Equipment & Magic Items**) that the high priestess placed here as a ruse to hide it in plain sight. A vision revealed to her that a dragon-like creature would soon come to the temple. She purchased the arrow and placed it here in preparation for the expected attack.

T-3. High Priestess's Room

This personal shrine is where the high priestess conducts hours-long meditations each evening. The door is thick and locked, but not trapped.

The high priestess is presently in the oratorium (**Area T-7**). The statue by the door is merely another idol of Dagon. It is worth 500 gp if recovered intact but weighs 500 pounds. A beautiful mother-of-pearl screen at the back of the room (1,200 gp) conceals the entrance to a large closet where a variety of vestments and odd temple apparel are kept in storage. These include a crown made of coral (1,800 gp). A covered candelabrum with six orbs filled with glowing greenish liquid gives off light as a torch when uncovered (300 gp). A specially designed "wet chest" that can secure its contents so they are unaffected by the outside watery environment (200 gp) holds nothing. A bookcase contains 62 blocky tablets made of a strange, coral-like material that is very light and easy to engrave on. Etched on all four sides, most of them are writings (in abyssal) by the oracle herself. They are filled with prophecies and mad musings on the origin and future of various sea races and nations, but there are also several treatises on sea-demons and Dagon in particular. They are worth 2,000 gp to an interested sage. A six-foot-long narwhal horn is carved along its four twirling paths with magical scrimshaws. These constitute four magic scrolls: *protection from poison*, *find traps*, *hold person*, and *monster summoning I* (giant blowfish only, see **Appendix A: New Monsters**).
Blowfish (2): HD 4; **AC** 6[13]; **Atk** slam (1d6 + poison quills); **Move** 12 (swim); **Save** 13; **AL** N; **CL/XP** 4/120; **Special:** poison quills (save or paralyzed for 1d4 rounds). (see **Appendix A: New Monsters**)

Wicked Reconfiguration Machine

Known by the ancients as the "Flesh and Soul Reconfiguration Contrivance," this device was intended to enable users to permanently modify their physical and mental abilities. In this way they hoped to enhance the vigor of their race. The device is not perfect, and results vary. The user risks receiving a bane rather than a boon (see the chart below). To operate the device, the user stands before the mural and grasps a baton in each hand. With a loud hum, mysterious runes flash in concentric circles for a full round as energies build and take form. To influence the transformation, users may increase their chances of a beneficial result by making a saving throw. On a success, they can roll 1d4 and add that to the roll. On a failed save, the user subtracts 1d4 from the roll. (Note: A user is not required to make a saving throw to use the machine; it just allows them a chance to push the odds in their favor.) All transformations have an undersea component to them, i.e. "improved vision" improves sight by giving the user fish-like eyes. Changes are permanent unless noted. Each use consumes three charges from the attached battery. The battery that is currently connected has only 10 charges remaining.

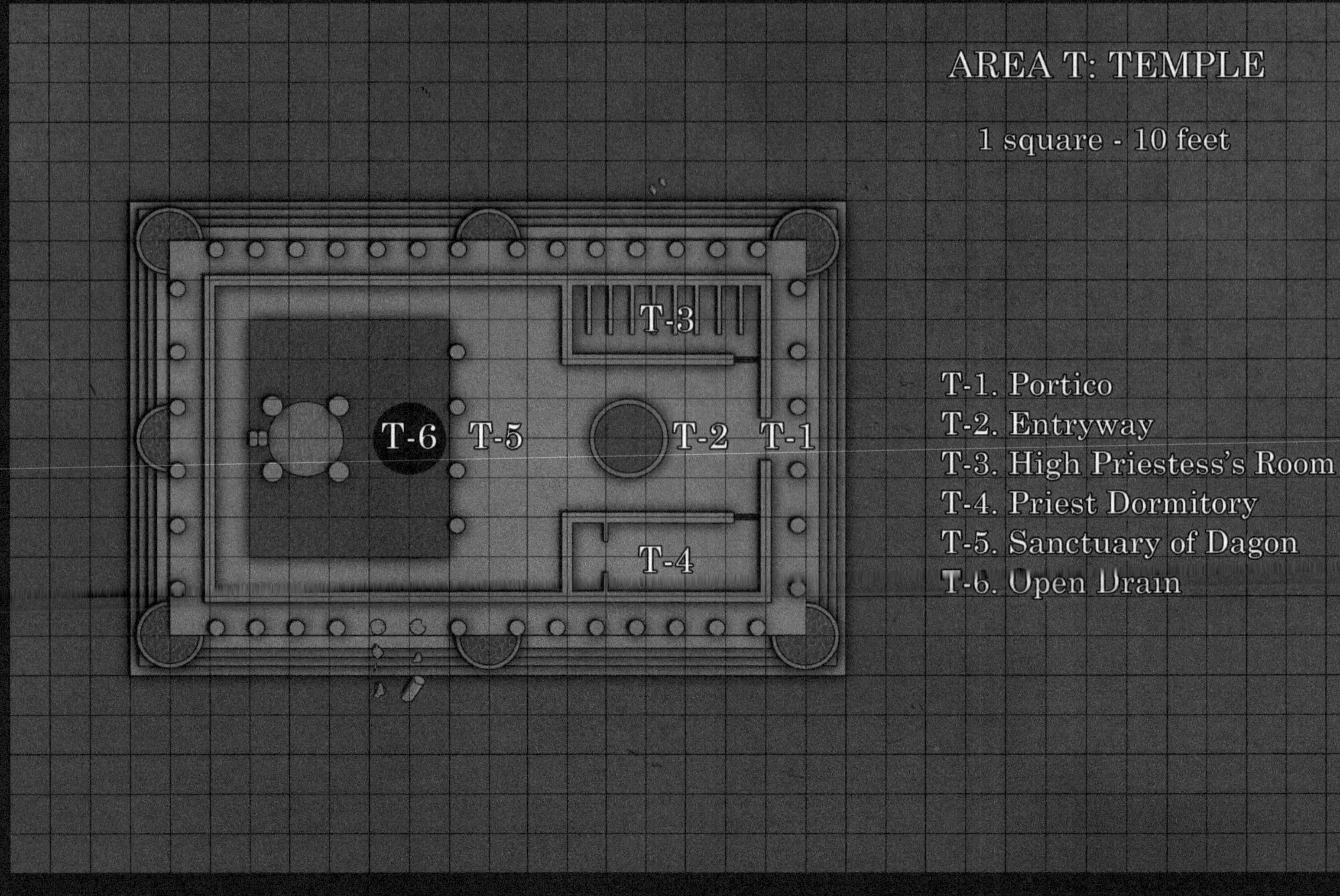

1d20	Banes and Boons
1	*Curse*: –6 penalty to random ability*
2	*Destruction*: Saving throw or die and rise as a **wraith**
3	Random energy vulnerability: cold/fire/acid/force/electricity (200% damage)
4	Saving throw or age d10 + 10 years
5	Saving throw or be polymorphed into a **giant leech**
6	*Reincarnation*: random race
7	Transformed into a **water elemental** for 24 hours*
8	Race changes to **skum**
9	Random ability score decreases by –1
10	Amorphous form (see **Area R-3. Shrine of Insanity**)
11	Ability score increases by +1 (choose one)
12	Permanent +1 bonus to saving throws
13	Gain darkvision (60 feet) or increase existing darkvision by 30 feet
14	Ability to cast *cure light wounds* once per day
15	*Reincarnation*: (choose race)
16	Ability to cast *strength* once per day
17	Ability to cast *lightning bolt* once per day that does 2d6 points of damage
18	Gain (1d4 + 1) x 1000 experience points
19+	User's choice (from above options)

* *Restoration* to remedy.

Giant Leech: HD 2; **AC** 3[16]; **Atk** bite (2d6); **Move** 6; **Save** 16; **AL** N; **CL/XP** 5/240; **Special:** sucks blood (1d4 damage/round). (see **Appendix A: New Monsters**)

Skum: Gain claw (1d4 damage) and bite (2d4 damage) attacks, and swim 12. (see **Appendix A: New Monsters**)

Water Elemental: HD 8; **AC** 2[17]; **Atk** strike (3d10); **Move** 6 (swim 18); **Save** 8; **AL** N; **CL/XP** 9/1100; **Special:** +1 or better magic weapons to hit, overturn boats (sink vessel in 1d4+4 rounds). (**Monstrosities** 157)

Wraith: HD 4; **AC** 3[16]; **Atk** touch (1d6 + level drain); **Move** 9 (fly 24); **Save** 13; **AL** C; **CL/XP** 8/800; **Special:** +1 or better magic or silver weapons to hit, level drain (1 level with hit). (**Monstrosities** 518)

T-4. PRIEST DORMITORY

Messy cots hide behind plain, dirty curtains that divide the space into nine semi-private apartments.

Air-breathing priestly minions of the temple bunk here. Of the eight current priests, **4 priests** are in this room. Four more are in **Area T-5**. These devotees of Dagon are drawn from local island populations. If the priests detect intruders, they suit up for combat and defend the temple.

These pale, clammy humans bear wicked-looking tridents and bear grim expressions. Their hair is long and unkempt, and their dirty wetsuits are made of studded leather.

If the priests are attacked here, they call out for the guards in the sanctuary. If they hear combat outside this room, they come out to support their comrades.

Priests of Dagon, Male or Female Humans or Elves (Clr4) (4): HP 23, 20, 17x2; **AC** 7[12]; **Atk** flail (1d8); **Move** 12; **Save** 12; **AL** C; **CL/XP** 4/120; **Special:** +2 save vs. paralysis and poison, banish undead, darkvision (60ft) (elves only), spells (2/1).

Spells: 1st—*cure light wounds* (x2); 2nd—*hold person.*

Equipment: leather armor, flail, holy symbol of Dagon.

T-5. SANCTUARY OF DAGON

A terrible idol of Dagon dominates the tall dais in the center of this magnificent chamber. The figure resembles a writhing mass of barbed, suckered tentacles cloaking a winding, eel-like body. Its head is that of a deep-sea fish with a baleful intelligence. Its toothy maw grins evilly. The ceiling soars to dark mosaics above. Tall support columns resemble bound stalks of seaweed rising from beds of coral. The sanctuary is covered in once beautiful bas-reliefs, but recent additions distort the images. Heads and limbs of figures have been reworked to resemble primordial sea creatures from some nightmarish Abyssal realm. A dark pool of water is before the idol. Four everburning flames in tall decorative braziers light the areas.

The ceiling rises 40 feet above the floor. A **skum warrior** named **Doolkah**, **4 skum** temple guards, and a **sahuagin priestess** named **Shacilla** ring the idol. The skum practice their worship music in the southwest corner of the room on drums, horns, and insanely constructed flutes. The instruments function in air and water environments and are worth 2,000 gp. Read the following:

Each scowling fish man wears a bronze helmet green with age. They pass a hand over odd-looking, tube-like devices at their hips that are attached by a line to a round metal shield of yellow metal. A magnetic whine begins, and each shield thrums with energy as the warriors draw deadly-looking tridents and take up practiced defensive stances.

The guards carry large round shields made of a special golden metal called orichalcum. Used by the ancients to channel their primordial magical energies, when attached to a special battery these orichalcum shields grant them a +1 bonus to their armor class. The batteries have limited charges. The ones used here have three charges remaining; each charge activates the armor class bonus for one turn. These same batteries can be used to power the wicked machine in **Area T-3**.

All creatures in this room fight bravely. If the temple looks as if it's under serious threat, Priestess Shacilla dives into the pool to alert the high priestess.

Doolkah, Skum Warrior: HD 6; HP 43; AC 3[16] or 2[17] while shield is activated; **Atk** *+1 trident* (1d6+1) or 2 claws (1d6), bite (2d4); **Move** 9 (swim 12); **Save** 11; **AL** C; **CL/XP** 6/400; **Special:** none. (see **Appendix A: New Monsters**)

Equipment: *orichalcum shield* [B], *+1 trident, potion of extra healing.*

Shacilla, Sahuagin Priestess: HD 7; HP 45; AC 5[14]; **Atk** *staff of striking* (2d6) or 2 claws (1d6), bite (2d4); **Move** 12 (swim 18); **Save** 9; **AL** C; **CL/XP** 7/600; **Special:** spells (2/2/2/1/1). (*Monstrosities* 407)

Spells: 1st—*cure light wounds, detect magic*; 2nd—*hold person* (x2); 3rd—*prayer, speak with dead*; 4th—*cure serious wounds*; 5th— *commune.*

Equipment: *staff of striking.*

Skum (4): HD 3; HP 23, 21, 17x2; AC 5[14]; **Atk** trident (1d6) or 2 claws (1d4), bite (2d4); **Move** 9 (swim 12); **Save** 14; **AL** C; **CL/XP** 3/60; **Special:** none. (see **Appendix A: New Monsters**)

Equipment: *orichalcum shield* [B], trident.

[B] See **Appendix B: Equipment & Magic Items**

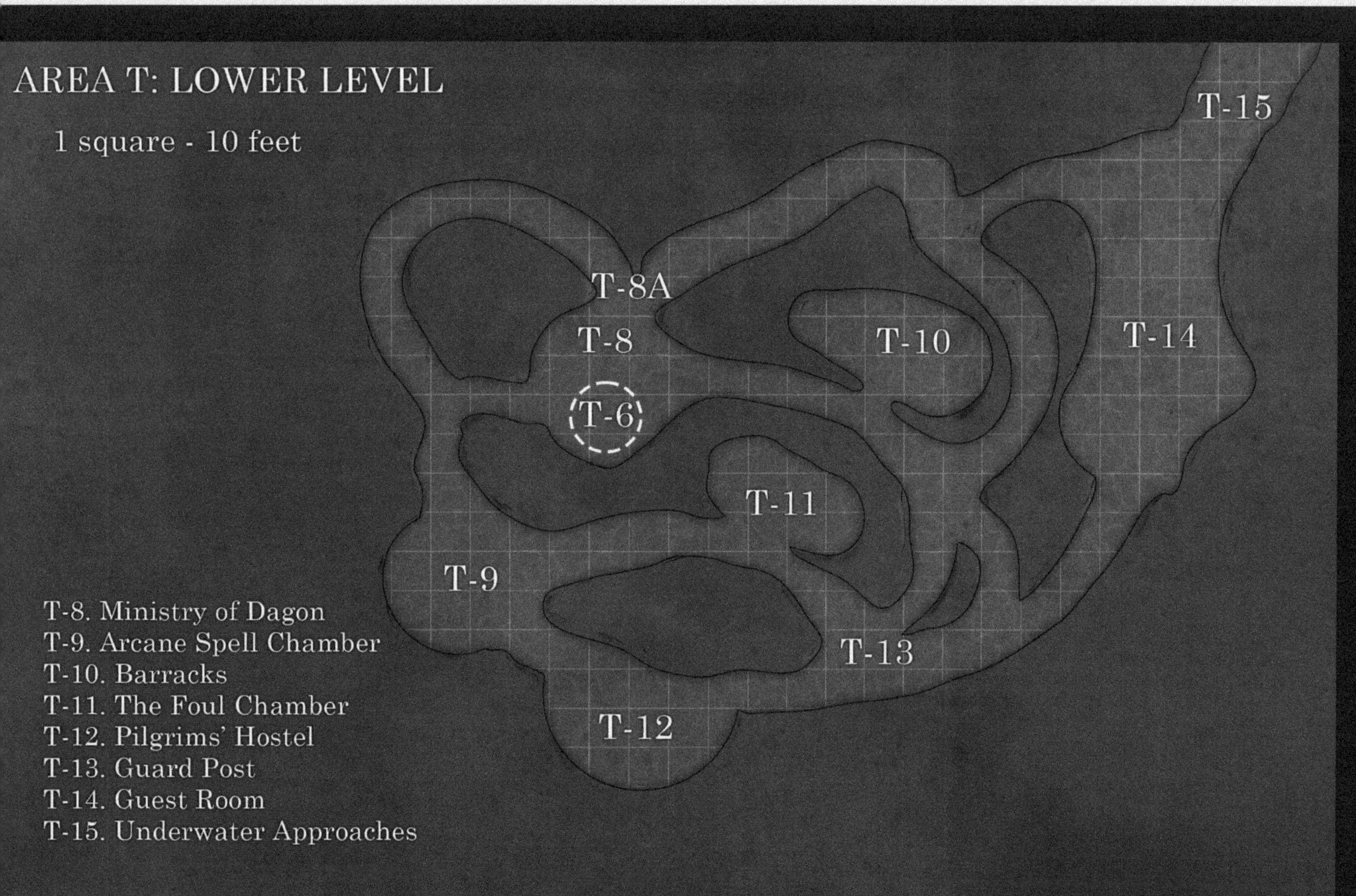

T-8. Ministry of Dagon
T-9. Arcane Spell Chamber
T-10. Barracks
T-11. The Foul Chamber
T-12. Pilgrims' Hostel
T-13. Guard Post
T-14. Guest Room
T-15. Underwater Approaches

The idol is trapped. Any living being who touches the idol awakens the Spirit of Dagon, which manifests as an illusion of the demon lord rising to attack. Read the following if anyone touches the statue:

> The gargantuan idol animates and reaches out for you, its many unblinking red eyes glaring and tentacles waving. Its maw is full of rows of long fangs, each dripping with slime, as it lunges out to devour you!

All creatures who witness the illusion must make a saving throw with a –2 penalty or believe the attack is real. They take 1d8 points of damage per round until they make a successful saving throw to disbelieve the illusion. *Dispel magic* ends the statue's "attacks."

T-6. Vertical Descent Passage

> A 10-foot-wide well at the bottom of the pool sinks into darkness. Glowing, rune-carved walls swirl downward, giving a dizzying sense of motion.

The tube descends 60 feet and opens into the ceiling of the ministry of Dagon (**Area T-8**). About halfway down, a side passage leads to the oratorium (**Area T-7**). Guarding the passage to the oratorium are **2 gray nisps** that attack strangers who enter the vertical passage. The runes carved on the walls are slightly nauseating, but otherwise harmless.

Gray Nisps (2): HD 8; HP 57, 48; AC 4[15]; Atk 2 claws (1d6), bite (1d8); Move 6 (swim 18); Save 8; AL C; CL/XP 8/800; Special: rend (if both claws hit target, additional 2d6 damage). (see **Appendix A: New Monsters**)

T-7. Oratorium

This encounter can be quite dangerous for an unprepared party, so carefully monitor their readiness and drop hints if necessary.

> The narrow passage opens into a glorious audience chamber with ramps ascending 20 feet on either side to the throne at the far end. Thin columns line the outer edges of the ramps, creating balconies along the run of the ramp that soar 40 feet to the ceiling. The ramps' ends flank a head of Dagon whose gaping maw is carved from the living rock of the chamber. Glowing blue stones cast an otherworldly light from the monster's eyes.

Lycinia, the temple's high priestess, spends much of her time in this room scheming and giving speeches to **4 lacedon** temple attendants. Carvings of ancient runes are on the walls of the tubular entryway. They are litanies on the glory of Dagon but are not dangerous. However, a magical glyph is carved at the threshold of the oratorium. Any Lawful or Neutral creature who crosses the threshold is affected by *dispel magic*. Lycinia is a fanatic and fights to the death.

Lycinia, Dagon High Priestess, Sea Medusa (Clr7): HD 10; HP 71; AC 8[11]; Atk *+1 trident* (1d6+1) and snake-hair (lethal poison); Move 9 (swim 15); Save 5; AL C; CL/XP 12/2000; Special: gaze turns to stone, lethal poison (save or die), spells (Clr 2/2/2/1/1). (*Monstrosities* 324)

Spells: 1st—*cure light wounds, detect magic*; 2nd—*bless, hold person*; 3rd—*continual light, prayer*; 4th—*cure serious wounds*; 5th—*finger of death*.

Equipment: *+1 trident*, unholy symbol of Dagon.

Lacedons (Aquatic Ghouls) (4): HD 2; HP 14, 12x2, 9; AC 6[13]; Atk 2 claws (1d3 + paralysis), bite (1d4); Move 9 (swim 12); Save 16; AL C; CL/XP 3/60; Special: immunities (charm and sleep), paralyzing touch (3d6 turns, save avoids). (*Monstrosities* 191)

T-8. Ministry of Dagon

This area includes the intersection at the bottom of the vertical shaft and the tubular passage to the northwest. Dozing here are **2 aquatic trolls**. Ever hungry, they attack any intruders when roused but they retreat to the barracks (**Area T-10**) or the guard post (**Area T-13**) for help if reduced to fewer than half their hit points. They fear the "ministers" to the northwest and the dragon in the guest room (**Area T-14**) and will not trespass in either of those places.

Aquatic Trolls (2): HD 6+3; HP 46, 40; AC 4[15]; Atk 2 claws (1d4), bite (1d8); **Move** 12; **Save** 11; **AL** C; **CL/XP** 8/800; **Special:** amphibious, regenerate (3hp/round). (*Monstrosities* 489)

A pair of alien scholars reside down the horseshoe-shaped tubal passageway to the northwest (**Area T-8A**), where they ponder the foul glories of Dagon. Abominations of mysterious origin, other temple devotees know them as the "ministers of Dagon" though they refer to themselves as **cnidarians**. They resemble enormous jellyfish with prehensile tentacles and throbbing blue brains deep within their blobby bodies. They appear to communicate with each other through hums and vibrations but with other creatures by marking on basalt tablets with a stylus. Though they have yet to produce much of any practical use, Lycinia places a high value on them. Hence, others in the temple give them a wide berth.

Ministers of Dagon, Cnidarians (2): HD 8; HP 57, 49; AC 6[13]; Atk 2 tentacles (1d6 + poison); **Move** 12 (swim) or jet (swim 27); **Save** 8; **AL** C; **CL/XP** 9/1100; **Special:** daze (1/day, 15ft radius, save or immobilized for 1d6+2 rounds), jet (blast water for movement rate 27), poison (save or flesh rots for 1d4 damage per round until healed). (see **Appendix A: New Monsters**)

The ministers ignore any noises or disturbances outside their passageway. They are far too absorbed in their studies to care. However, if attacked, they use their daze ability and tentacle attacks. Their daze is a kind of overwhelming telepathic feedback to distract and confuse opponents, blasting them with words and information. If attacked from one direction, one of them swims around to the other side and attacks the party from behind.

Seven hand-sized idols of ancient gods expertly carved from coral and worth 50 gp each are on shelf-like niches in the tubular passage. Two of them contain magical liquids: a *potion of barnacleskin* and a *potion of fins to feet* (see **Appendix B: Equipment & Magic Items** for both).

Despite its appearance, the writing on the walls (mostly in aboleth) is not magical. The glowing letters are achieved using rare undersea pigments. Several rubbings can be obtained from the writing. It takes time (10 minutes per section) but 10 sections can be copied for a trade value of 1,000 gp each.

T-9. Arcane Spell Chamber

This room constitutes a massive spellbook containing 2d4 magic-user spells, 4d4 cleric spells, and 1d4 druid spells. Choose the spells or roll randomly to determine what the characters find. Though written in an ancient script, each spell can be accurately interpreted. If the glyphs are touched, a **trilobite swarm** is summoned and attacks.

Swarm of Trilobites: HD 6; HP 41; AC 4[15]; Atk swarm (2d6); **Move** 9 (swim 18); **Save** 11; **AL** N; **CL/XP** 6/400; **Special:** none. (see **Appendix A: New Monsters**)

A locked secret door is in the floor. Beneath is a 30-foot-wide spherical room warded to prevent its single occupant from leaving. This encounter is optional because it is extremely dangerous. Include it only if you determine it is a fair challenge for the characters.

The Foul Chamber

The high priestess keeps **G'zhool**, a **hezrou demon**, inside this 30-foot-wide chamber. Summoned for some nefarious future plan, his reeking body is too unpleasant for most of the water-breathing denizens of the temple to endure for long. Thus, he is kept imprisoned in this room. Bored with his detention, the demon happily attacks any intruder foolish enough to open the door, although he prefers to wait until they enter before attacking. Remember that this room is like a spherical fishbowl entered from above; those who can't swim may sink to the bottom, possibly putting themselves out of melee range. He fights until he sees an opportunity to charge out of the room. If brought to 0 hit points, he bursts into oily, black slime, leaving only his necklace behind. The room is unremarkable except for the smell. G'zhool wears a surprisingly beautiful gold medallion crafted into a likeness of Dagon (2,000 gp). It hangs around his neck on a chain of thick silver links (1,000 gp).

G'zhool, Second-Category Demon (Hezrou Type): HD 9; HP 63; AC –2[21]; Atk 2 claws (1d3), bite (4d4); **Move** 6 (fly 12); **Save** 6; **AL** C; **CL/XP** 11/1700; **Special:** immune to fire, magic resistance (50%), spell-like abilities, summon demons (20% chance, hezrou). (*Monstrosities* 96)

Spell-like abilities: at will—*darkness 15ft radius, detect invisibility, fear.*

T-10. Skum Barracks

The room is the bunk space for **6 skum** temple guards. They switch off with the guards in the main sanctuary (**Area T-1**) or at the guard posts in the lower levels (**Areas T-13** and **T-15**). Those found here are likely sleeping. Each has weapons and armor bound in a nearby net.

Skum Guards (6): HD 3; HP 21, 19x2, 17, 15x2; AC 5[14]; Atk trident (1d6) or 2 claws (1d4), bite (2d4); **Move** 9 (swim 12); **Save** 14; **AL** C; **CL/XP** 3/60; **Special:** none. (see **Appendix A: New Monsters**)

T-11. Litharium

To unlock the door, the pieces must be realigned to form the rough image of an aboleth. Characters can solve the puzzle by rolling below their intelligence on 4d6. If unlocked, the stone door rolls to the side and allows entrance. Any failure sets off a trap. If the trap is triggered, jets of freezing water shoot out from the frame of the doorway. Each creature within the chamber must make a saving throw. A creature that fails takes 2d6 points of cold damage and is restrained by the ice. A creature that succeeds takes half this damage and is not restrained. A restrained creature can attempt an Open Doors check each round to escape, but takes an additional 1d6 points of damage each round they remain trapped. If they don't succeed before, the ice releases them after 10 minutes. The trap takes one hour to reset.

The ancients stored rare gemstones here. The drawers contain 52 stones of various sizes. If collected, the gems are worth a total of 1d100 x 200 gp.

T-12. Pilgrims' Hostel

Crossbows, bolt cases, tridents, spears, and weapon belts hang from hooks on the walls. Large sewn seaweed duffels used like sleeping bags are lined up at the back of the room.

Camped out in this room are **8 sahuagin** and **2 sharks**. They are waiting to attend the next weekly sacrificial ceremony. They brought a box of treasure and two sea elf captives as offerings to Dagon. The leader also carries a *pearl of the sirens* (see **Appendix B: Equipment & Magic Items**). A sahuagin leads his sharks around to the rear of an invading force to attack from behind — alerting temple guards as he finds them. The box is unlocked and contains a variety of valuables from sunken ships (cups, plates, rings, etc.) worth 1,000 gp. Any treasure not part of the ancient site is fair salvage for the party and does not need to be turned in. However, it is still accepted for credit if desired at the same rate.

Sahuagins (8): HD 2+1; HP 17, 15x2, 14, 12, 11, 10, 8; AC 5[14]; Atk spear (1d8); Move 12 (swim 18); Save 16; AL C; CL/XP 2/30; Special: none. (*Monstrosities* 407)

Sharks (2): HD 4; HP 27, 23; AC 6[13]; Atk bite (1d4+1); Move 0 (swim 24); Save 13; AL N; CL/XP 4/120; Special: feeding frenzy (1-in-6 chance of attacking another shark). (*Monstrosities* 420)

Sea Elves (2): HD 1+1; HP 3, 2; AC 5[14]; Atk longsword (1d8), Move 12 (swim 12); Save 17; AL L; CL/XP 1/15; Special: darkvision (60ft), find secret doors (4-in-6 chance), immune to ghoul paralysis. (*Monstrosities* 159)

T-13. Guard Post

The tube-like passage widens and flattens at an intersection. Sections of the wall contain half-completed carvings depicting grotesque sea creatures menacing hapless human swimmers.

Keeping watch at this point are **3 skum** temple guards. If they notice a dangerous group of intruders, they retreat to alert the guards in the skum barracks (**Area T-10**) or the high priestess in the oratorium (**Area T-7**).

Skum Guards (3): HD 3; HP 20, 17, 15; AC 5[14] or 2[17] with *octopus shield*; Atk trident (1d6) or 2 claws (1d4), bite (2d4); Move 9 (swim 12); Save 14; AL C; CL/XP 3/60; Special: none. (see **Appendix A: New Monsters**)

Note: One of the guards has an *octopus shield* (see **Appendix B: Equipment & Magic Items**) that gives it AC 2[17] and lets it grab opponents up to 10 feet away three times per day if they fail a saving throw. An Open Doors check is required to break free of the tentacles.

T-14. Guest Room

An **adult black dragon** named Distrattadora recently arrived to pay tribute to Dagon and join the gathering forces for plunder. She is patiently awaiting her audience with the high priestess. If she detects intruders, she is annoyed at the disturbance and the lack of proper security. She breaks her pose and cheerfully blasts the intruders with her breath weapon before entering melee.

Distrattadora does not believe any intruders could possibly threaten her life, but if she is reduced to half her hit points, she roars angrily in hopes of summoning help from the guards at the guard post (**Area T-13**), who arrive in one round. If they see it's hopeless, they retreat to the ministry of Dagon (**Area T-8**) to alert the aquatic trolls and also send one of their number to warn the high priestess (**Area T-7**). See the **Temple Tactics** sidebar for more information.

Distrattadora carries treasure with her in belt bags (7,000 gp in coin, gold jewelry, and pearls). If the ceiling is searched, a hovering belt buckle can be found. It is made of orichalcum. Long ago, sculptors used it as a brace for underwater carving. If the belts are reconstructed and the activation words discovered, it functions as a belt that suspends the wearer in any environment.

Distrattadora, Female Adult Black Dragon: HD 7; HP 28; AC 2[17]; Atk 2 claws (1d4), bite (3d6); Move 9 (fly 24); Save 9; AL C; CL/XP 6/1100; Special: spits acid (3/day, 60ft line, 28 damage, save for half). (*Monstrosities* 132)

T-15. Underwater Approach

Ranging near the underwater entrance are **4 devilfish** that remain concealed behind a grove of seaweed at the base of the temple mount. They are aggressive and attack suspicious characters. Standing guard just inside the opening are **2 skum** temple guards. If faced with a well-armed force, they retreat inside to warn the high priestess. See the **Temple Tactics** sidebar below for more.

Devilfish (4): HD 5; HP 33, 30, 27, 22; AC 5[14]; Atk 3 tentacles (1d6+2 + grapple), bite (2d6+2); Move 3 (swim 15); Save 12; AL C; CL/XP 6/400; Special: grapple (save after strike or held, automatic bite damage until freed), resists cold (50% damage), unholy blood (1/day, emit cloud, 20ft radius, save or poisoned, −2 to hit, saves, and damage for 1d6 rounds). (see **Appendix A: New Monsters**)

Skum Guards (2): HD 3; HP 19, 17; AC 5[14]; Atk trident (1d6) or 2 claws (1d4), bite (2d4); Move 9 (swim 12); Save 14; AL C; CL/XP 3/60; Special: none. (see **Appendix A: New Monsters**)

If the sunken ruins are cleared of monsters before an assault on the temple, then the temple inhabitants are more on their guard. Murder and mayhem is commonplace among the motley assemblage of creatures in the ruins, so minor disturbances go unheeded. As well, defeated denizens of the ruins are also unlikely to report their losses to the high priestess. Chaotic Dagonians are not known for their support and compassion.

The inhabitants of the temple don't just sit around once they become aware that the complex is under attack. If adventurers are noticed entering from the underwater approach passage (**Area T-15**), guards in **Areas T-11** and **T-13** are alerted and one of their number swims off to alert the high priestess (**Area T-7**). She takes her lacedon bodyguards to the bottom of the vertical passage (**Area T-6**) and moves to assail the intruders. If hard pressed, Lycinia summons aid from the aquatic trolls and "ministers" in **Area T-8** and directs them to circle around from a new direction to surround the invaders. If possible, she attempts to capture prisoners to interrogate. If alerted that the temple sanctuary (**Areas T-2** through **T-5**) is under attack, she prepares her defenses in **Area T-7**. She sends one lacedon to summon the aquatic trolls in **Area T-8** to take a defensive position in the entry hall to the oratorium (**Area T-7**).

EPILOGUE

If at any point High Priestess Lycinia is slain, word spreads quickly and her minions in the dungeon or sunken ruins quickly leave the area to seek their fortunes elsewhere. Without a charismatic spiritual leader at the center of the community, the remaining skum and sahuagin break ranks. Human cultists flee in terror, taking anything of value that they can carry. The remaining monsters, including the hag coven and Distrattadora the black dragon, lurk around the complex and can still be encountered.

APPENDIX A: NEW MONSTERS

ALLIP

Hit Dice: 4
Armor Class: 5[14]
Attacks: strike (no damage, 1d4 wisdom drain)
Saving Throw: 13
Special: Drains wisdom, hypnosis
Move: 6 (fly)
Alignment: Chaos
Number Encountered: 1, 1d3
Challenge Level: 7/600

Allips are shadowy, incorporeal undead that mutter and speak with the voice of madness from beyond the grave. Their voice acts as a *suggestion* spell upon anyone hearing the quiet mutterings; the suggestions of an allip are usually senseless but sinister. The allip's touch does not deal damage, but causes the victim to lose 1d4 points of wisdom. If a victim's wisdom falls to 0, it dies and becomes an allip within 2d6 days. Allips can be hit only with magical or silver weapons.

Allip: HD 4; AC 5[14]; **Atk** strike (no damage, drain wisdom); **Move** 6 (fly); **Save** 13; **AL** C; **CL/XP** 7/600; **Special:** +1 or better magic or silver weapon to hit, drain wisdom (1d4 points with hit), hypnosis (as *suggestion* spell).

ASSASSIN VINE

Hit Dice: 7
Armor Class: 5[14]
Attacks: Vine (1d6+1)
Saving Throw: 9
Special: Animate plants
Move: 1
Alignment: Neutrality
Number Encountered: 1 (subterranean) or 1d8 (aboveground)
Challenge Level: 8/800

The assassin vine is a semi-mobile plant that collects its own grisly fertilizer by grabbing and crushing animals and depositing the carcasses near its roots. A mature plant consists of a main vine that is about 20 feet long. Smaller vines, up to five feet long, branch off from the main vine about every six inches. An assassin vine can move about, albeit very slowly, but usually stays put unless it needs to seek prey in a new vicinity.

An assassin vine growing underground usually generates enough offal to support a thriving colony of mushrooms and other fungi, which spring up around the plant and help conceal it.

An assassin vine can animate plants in the near vicinity (about 30 feet), and these plants immobilize anyone failing a saving throw.

Assassin Vine: HD 7; AC 5[14]; **Atk** vine (1d6+1); **Move** 1; **Save** 9; **AL** N; **CL/XP** 8/800; **Special:** animate plants (30ft range, immobilize any creature that fails a saving throw).

CARYATID COLUMN

Hit Dice: 5
Armor Class: 5[14]
Attacks: Longsword (1d8+1)
Saving Throw: 12
Special: Immune to magic, resist normal weapons (50% damage), shatter weapons
Move: 9
Alignment: Neutrality
Number Encountered: 1d4
Challenge Level: 7/600

A caryatid column is akin to the stone golem in that it is a magical construct created by a spellcaster. They look like exquisitely sculpted and chiseled statues of beautiful female warriors carrying longswords. The longsword is constructed of steel, but is melded with the column and made of stone until the column animates. Caryatid columns are programmed as guardians and activate when certain conditions or stipulations are met or broken (such as a living creature enters a chamber guarded by a caryatid column). It does not move more than 50 feet from the area it is guarding or protecting. They are immune to all spells except *transmute rock to mud*, which deals 1d6 points of damage per caster level to the caryatid column, *transmute mud to rock*, which heals the caryatid column of all damage and *stone to flesh*, which makes it subject to normal damage from weapons and suspends its immunity to magic for 1 round. Whenever a weapon strikes the caryatid column, the wielder must pass a saving throw or the weapon shatters into pieces. Magic weapons add their enchantment bonus to the saving throw.

Caryatid Column: HD 5; AC 5[14]; **Atk** longsword (1d8+1); **Move** 9; **Save** 12; **AL** N; **CL/XP** 7/600; **Special:** immune to magic (except *transmute rock to mud* [1d6 damage per level], *transmute mud to rock* [heals all damage], *stone to flesh* [subject to normal damage and magic for 1 round]), resist normal weapons (50% damage), shatter weapons (weapon that hits must save or be destroyed).

CNIDARIAN

Hit Dice: 8
Armor Class: 6[13]
Attacks: 2 tentacles (1d6 + poison)
Saving Throw: 8
Special: Daze, jet, poison
Move: 6 (swim) or jet (swim 27)
Alignment: Chaos
Number Encountered: 1d4
Challenge Level: 9/1,100

Cnidarians resemble enormous jellyfish with prehensile tentacles
and throbbing blue brains deep within their blobby bodies. They
communicate with each other through hums and vibrations. They
use their tentacles to mark on basalt tablets with a stylus to speak
with other creatures. A cnidarian attacks with two tentacles that
deliver a poison that rots flesh. Any creature struck by a tentacle
must make a saving throw or take 1d4 points of damage each
round until healed. Once per day, a cnidarian can unleash a blast
of energy. All creatures within 15 feet of the cnidarian must make
a saving throw or be dazed and unable to move for 1d6+2 rounds. A
cnidarian can jet water to achieve a movement rate of 27 to escape
danger.

Cnidarian: HD 8; AC 6[13]; **Atk** 2 tentacles (1d6 + poison); **Move**
12 (swim) or jet (swim 27); **Save** 8; **AL** C; **CL/XP** 9/1100; **Special:**
daze (1/day, 15ft radius, save or immobilized for 1d6+2 rounds), jet
(blast water for movement rate 27), poison (save or flesh rots for 1d4
damage per round until healed).

CRYSTAL OOZE

Hit Dice: 4
Armor Class: 7[12]
Attacks: Strike (2d6 + paralysis)
Saving Throw: 13
Special: Acid, immunities, paralysis, transparent, water dependent
Move: 3/6 (swim)
Alignment: Neutrality
Number Encountered: 1d2
Challenge Level: 6/400

The crystal ooze is an aquatic variety of the gray ooze. It is
semitransparent and clear, almost impossible to see in the water,
and looks like nothing more than a puddle of water. The crystal
ooze can grow to a length of up to eight feet with a thickness of
about six inches.

A crystal ooze secretes a digestive acid that quickly dissolves organic
material, but not metal. Half of the damage from a melee hit is
from this acid. Non-metal armor or clothing dissolves and becomes
useless immediately unless its wearer succeeds on a saving
throw. A wooden weapon that strikes a crystal ooze also dissolves
immediately unless the wielder succeeds on a saving throw.

In addition to its digestive acid, a crystal ooze secretes a paralytic
slime. A target hit by a crystal ooze's strike must succeed on a
saving throw or be paralyzed for 3d6 rounds. Crystal oozes can
survive out of the water for five hours.

Crystal Ooze: HD 4; AC 7[12]; **Atk** strike (2d6 + paralysis);
Move 3 (swim 6); **Save** 13; **AL** N; **CL/XP** 6/400; **Special:**
acid (dissolve organic material), immunities (acid, cold,
fire), paralysis (save or paralyzed for 3d6 rounds),
transparent (20% chance to spot in water), water
dependent (dies after five hours out of water).

DEVILFISH

Hit Dice: 5
Armor Class: 5[14]
Attacks: 3 tentacles (1d6+2 + grapple), bite (2d6+2)
Saving Throw: 12
Special: Grapple, resist cold, unholy blood
Move: 3/15 (swim)
Alignment: Chaos
Number Encountered: 1d6, 2d4
Challenge Level: 6/400

A devilfish is a 10- to 12-foot-long creature similar to an octopus or
squid with seven tentacles. They attack with up to three barbed
tentacles that radiate around their central body. The creature has
a powerful beak that can deliver a deadly bite. They cannot survive
long out of water. A devilfish's blood is infused with fiendish magic.
Once per day, it can emit a night-black cloud of this foul liquid,
filling a 20-foot-radius cloud if underwater, or a 20-foot-radius burst
on land. In water, this cloud acts as *darkness 20-foot radius*. Any
creature caught in the cloud (or struck by the burst on land) must
make a saving throw or be poisoned and suffer a –2 penalty to hit,
damage, and saves for 1d6 rounds.

Devilfish: HD 5; AC 5[14]; **Atk** 3 tentacles (1d6+2 + grapple), bite
(2d6+2); **Move** 3 (swim 15); **Save** 12; **AL** C; **CL/XP** 6/400; **Special:**
grapple (save after strike or held, automatic bite damage until
freed), resists cold (50% damage), unholy blood (1/day, emit cloud,
20ft radius, save or poisoned, –2 to hit, saves, and damage for 1d6
rounds).

Eye of the Deep

Hit Dice: 10
Armor Class: 4[15]
Attacks: Eye rays (see below), 2 pincers (2d4), bite (1d6)
Saving Throw: 5
Special: Constrict, eye rays, stun cone
Move: 3/9 (swim)
Alignment: Chaos
Number Encountered: 1d3
Challenge Level: 13/2,300

The eye of the deep is a five-foot-wide orb dominated by a central eye and a large serrated mouth. Hundreds of small, seaweed-like bristles hang from the bottom of its body. Two large crab-like pincers protrude from its body, and two long, thin eyestalks sprout from the top of its orb. Eyes of the deep are found only in the deepest parts of the ocean, though on occasion one moves too close to the shoreline and ends up beaching on the sands. An eye of the deep stranded in this manner dies in 2d4 minutes unless placed back into the water. Eyes of the deep speak their own language and the common tongue of seafaring humans.

Creatures struck by the eye of the deep's pincers must make a saving throw or be caught and crushed for 2d4 points of automatic damage each round until they can pry open those pincers with an Open Doors check.

Each of the creature's eyes stalks can produce a magical ray once per round. The creature can aim both of its eye rays in any direction. Each of its eye rays resembles a spell cast by a 12th-level caster and requires a ranged attack (ignores armor) to hit. Each eye ray has a range of 150 feet. The left eye emits a *hold person* ray, while the right eye emits a *hold monster* ray. By combining both eye rays, the eye of the deep can replicate the *phantasmal force* spell.

An eye of the deep's central eye can, once per round, produce a cone extending straight ahead from its front to a range of 30 feet. Creatures in the area must succeed on a saving throw or be stunned for 2d4 rounds.

Eye of the Deep: HD 10; AC 4[15]; Atk 2 pincers (2d4 + constrict), bite (1d6); **Move** 3 (swim 9); **Save** 5; AL C; CL/XP 13/2300; **Special:** constrict (after pincer hit, save or held, automatic 2d4 damage per round, Open Doors check to escape), eye rays (attack as 12th-level caster, ranged attack to hit, 150ft range, 1 each/round [hold person, hold monster] or 1/round [phantasmal force]), stun cone (central eye, 30ft cone, 1/round [save or stunned for 2d4 rounds]).

Giant Blowfish

Hit Dice: 4
Armor Class: 6[13]
Attacks: Slam (1d6 + poison quills)
Saving Throw: 13
Special: Poison quills
Move: 12 (swim)
Alignment: Neutrality
Number Encountered: 1d4
Challenge Level: 4/120

The blowfish is a three-foot-long fish that can inflate itself to scare away predators. It is covered in sharp quills that secrete a paralytic poison. Any creature within five feet of the fish when it instantly expands must make a saving throw or be struck by 1d4 quills that do 1d3 points of damage each. Any creature struck by a quill must make a saving throw or be paralyzed for 1d4 rounds. The blowfish slams into enemies, which forces them to make a saving throw against the poison.

Blowfish: HD 4; AC 6[13]; Atk slam (1d6 + poison quills); **Move** 12 (swim); **Save** 13; AL N; CL/XP 4/120; **Special:** poison quills (save or paralyzed for 1d4 rounds).

Giant Leech

Hit Dice: 2
Armor Class: 3[16]
Attacks: Bite (2d6)
Saving Throw: 16
Special: Suck blood
Move: 6
Alignment: Neutrality
Number Encountered: 1d4
Challenge Level: 5/240

Giant leeches are about one and a half feet long per hit die. After they hit, they drain blood automatically at 1d4 points of damage per round. These are nasty creatures to find inhabiting the murky, muddy waters of a dungeon or swamp.

Giant Leech: HD 2; AC 3[16]; Atk bite (2d6); **Move** 6; **Save** 16; AL N; CL/XP 5/240; **Special:** sucks blood (1d4 damage/round). (*Monstrosities* 289)

Giant Moray Eel

Hit Dice: 4
Armor Class: 7[12]
Attacks: Bite (2d6)
Saving Throw: 13
Special: None
Move: 0/9 (swim)
Alignment: Neutrality
Number Encountered: 1d4
Challenge Level: 4/120

The giant moray eel is about 10 feet long. Larger eels might have greater hit dice. Moray eels attack with a vicious bite.

Giant Moray Eel: HD 4; AC 7[12]; Atk bite (2d6); **Move** 0 (swim 9); **Save** 13; AL N; CL/XP 4/120; **Special:** none.

Giant Sea Anemone, Immature

Hit Dice: 8
Armor Class: 8[11]
Attacks: Tendrils (paralysis)
Saving Throw: 8
Special: Acid cloud, paralytic poison, swallow whole
Move: 0 (immobile)
Alignment: Neutrality
Number Encountered: 1d4
Challenge Level: 8/800

This flowerlike creature has a dark green to gray trunk and a brightly colored interior. At the center of the creature's front is a circular opening that leads into its interior. An anemone attacks any creature that swims into its many tendrils with a paralytic poison that immobilizes prey so it can be swallowed whole. A victim caught in the tendrils can save to resist the paralysis. If a creature fails the saving throw, the anemone swallows the prey whole in the next round. If provoked, an anemone ejects the contents of its stomach in an acidic cloud that deals 1d8 points of damage to all creatures within 20 feet for 1d3 rounds.

Sea Anemone, Giant (Immature): HD 8; AC 8[11]; Atk tendrils (paralysis); **Move** 0 (immobile); **Save** 8; AL N; CL/XP 8/800; **Special:** acid cloud (1d8 damage for 1d3 rounds to all within 20 feet radius), paralytic poison (save or immobilized), swallow whole (immobilized creatures).

Gray Nisp

Hit Dice: 8
Armor Class: 4[15]
Attacks: 2 claws (1d6), bite (1d8)
Saving Throw: 8
Special: Rend
Move: 6/18 (swim)
Alignment: Chaos
Number Encountered: 1d4, 2d6
Challenge Level: 8/800

Gray nisps are hairless humanoids with smooth, slick skin. Their hands and feet are webbed and end in claws, and their faces have large, dark, pupil-less eyes. They have no noses or ears, and their small fishlike mouths are filled with tiny, sharp teeth. Gray nisps are nine feet tall, with light gray skin and a white underbelly, and weigh well over 300 pounds. If a gray nisp hits with both claws, it rends for an additional 2d6 points of damage. A gray nisp cannot survive on dry land.

Gray Nisp: HD 8; **AC** 4[15]; **Atk** 2 claws (1d6), bite (1d8); **Move** 6 (swim 18); **Save** 8; **AL** C; **CL/XP** 8/800; **Special:** rend (if both claws hit target, additional 2d6 damage).

Skum

Hit Dice: 3
Armor Class: 5[14]
Attacks: Trident (1d6) or 2 claws (1d4), bite (2d4)
Saving Throw: 14
Special: None
Move: 9/12 (swim)
Alignment: Chaos
Number Encountered: 1d3, 2d6
Challenge Level: 3/60

Skum are hunchbacked, green-skinned humanoid predators that lurk beneath the waves. They have a frog-like head with a large tooth-filled mouth. They can breathe air and water, but begin to suffocate if they don't submerge at least once every four hours. They attack with a trident, or their claws and vicious bite.

Skum: HD 3; **AC** 5[14]; **Atk** trident (1d6) or 2 claws (1d4), bite (2d4); **Move** 9 (swim 12); **Save** 14; **AL** C; **CL/XP** 3/60; **Special:** none.

Skum Warrior: HD 5; **AC** 3[16]; **Atk** *+1 trident* (1d6+1) or 2 claws (1d6), bite (2d4); **Move** 9 (swim 12); **Save** 12; **AL** C; **CL/XP** 5/240; **Special:** none.

      Equipment: *+1 trident, potion of extra healing.*

Swarm of Trilobites

Hit Dice: 6
Armor Class: 4[15]
Attacks: Swarm (2d6)
Saving Throw: 11
Special: None
Move: 9/18 (swim)
Alignment: Neutrality
Number Encountered: 1d3
Challenge Level: 6/400

A swarm of trilobites contains hundreds of tiny primeval crab-like creatures that bite and claw creatures as they strip flesh from bone.

Swarm of Trilobites: HD 6; **AC** 4[15]; **Atk** swarm (2d6); **Move** 9 (swim 18); **Save** 11; **AL** N; **CL/XP** 6/400; **Special:** none.

APPENDIX B: EQUIPMENT & MAGIC ITEMS

Listed below are new mundane and magical items found in this adventure:

Miscellaneous Magical Items, Greater

Carpet of Holding

A *carpet of holding* appears to be a five-foot-by-10-foot area rug with ornate designs. If an item is placed on the carpet and the carpet is then folded or rolled up, the item shifts into a nondimensional space capable of holding up to 1,000 pounds and 150 cubic feet. When the command word is spoken and the carpet unfolded, the contents appear again just as they were before. If the carpet is merely unfolded without speaking the command word, it appears and functions as an ordinary carpet, at which point new objects up to the maximum weight may be added as desired.

A living creature placed within the closed carpet can survive for up to 10 minutes, after which time they suffocate. If a *carpet of holding* is placed within a *portable hole*, a rift to the Astral Plane is torn asunder in the space. The carpet and the *portable hole* are sucked into the void and lost forever. Attempting to place a *portable hole* or a *bag of holding* in a folded *carpet of holding* repels the magic items away from the carpet with magnetic force and prevents the carpet from closing.

Decanter of Endless Air

This stoppered flask weighs about one pound. You can remove the stopper and speak one of three command words, whereupon a quantity of fresh air comes streaming out. The air stops flowing at the start of your next turn. Choose from the following options:

* "Breath" produces enough air for you to breathe deeply, filling your lungs.
* "Gust" produces a 10-foot stream of air that is strong enough to extinguish small flames, fan large flames, and move light objects.
* "Tempest" produces a powerful wind that is 30 feet long and one foot wide. While holding the decanter, you can aim the wind at a creature you can see within 30 feet of you. The target must succeed on a saving throw or take 1d4 points of damage and be knocked down. Instead, you can target an object that isn't being worn or carried and that weighs no more than 200 pounds. The object is either knocked over or pushed up to 15 feet away from you.

Helm of Water Breathing

While wearing this helm underwater, you can speak its command word to cause the helm to provide you with air to breathe. It continues to provide you with fresh air until you speak the command word again, the helm is removed, or you are no longer underwater.

Miscellaneous Magical Item, Medium

Pearl of the Sirens

While holding this pearl in your hand, you can breathe underwater, you gain a swim movement rate of 12, and you can cast spells and act underwater without hindrance.

Missile Weapon

Arrow of Dragon Slaying

An *arrow of dragon slaying* is a deadly arrow if used against a dragon. If the arrow successful strikes a dragon, the creature must make a saving throw or instantly die. Even if the creature succeeds on the save, it still takes 4d6 points of damage from the strike.

Potions

Potion of Barnacleskin

When you drink this potion, your skin becomes covered in barnacles. If you are not wearing armor, you gain a –2[+2] bonus to your armor class. The effect lasts for one hour.

Potion of Fins to Feet

When you drink this potion, you gain the ability to breathe air and you can transform your body to have humanoid legs. You gain a walking movement rate equal to your swim speed. The effect lasts for 4 hours. If a creature with legs drinks the potion, nothing happens, although there is a 10% chance that the creature's legs fuse into a tail like that of the merfolk.

Potion of Water Breathing

When you drink this potion, you gain the ability to breathe underwater for one hour.

Shield

Octopus Shield

This round, heavy bronze and steel shield is fashioned to resemble a raging octopus. You gain a –2[+2] bonus to your armor class in addition to the shield's normal bonus. Three times per day, you can cause the tentacles on the shield to lash out to grab opponents within 10 feet. Creatures must make a saving throw or be held (Open Doors check to escape). Only one creature can be held by the tentacles at a time.

BOUNTY

IN GOLD *For The Heads Of*

PIRATES

Attacking Trade Ships

&

Murdering Our People!

Our honorable High Judge

Percutio Opavian

Will issue

Letters of marque

To

Heroic Corsairs

Who take up the sword against our enemies

Present this notice to the Judicial Palace